BOSTON JONSON IN
MURDER BY COFFEE

Biff Mitchell

BOSTON JONSON IN
MURDER BY COFFEE

DOUBLE DRAGON

Chapter 1 - Let us begin...

It was a bustling place, crowded by late-night coffee swillers with throats like pipelines running high octane caffeine, but somehow they found a way to talk through the flow of java and they were all talking at the same time, drowning out the re-mixed jazz tunes from musicians who were mostly dried bones, which was mostly a good thing since they couldn't hear what the late 21st Century had done to their music. He guessed that most of the crowd were college students, meeting here with their holotops to work in groups on assignments from professors they'd never met in real life, eProfs who appeared as talking heads on their students' computers. The rest of the crowd looked like artists, writers and musicians who thought the digitally squeezed music actually said something. And then there were the coffee shop spooks, the ones who sat night after night guzzling into the wee hours because that's what they did. A few of them read books-print books, with paper pages.

Boston Jonson was looking at one of them now. She was a heavy woman, at least two hundred pounds, bent forward on a coffee high, book in one hand, the other grasping a porcelain cup between a massive thumb and index finger. She had that look of intensity that comes from reading too much, living in a world constructed by everybody but herself. And a connoisseur obviously-the print book in her plump hand was a hard bound with a glossy cover. They were rare. Most people used ereaders and holotops for interactive reading. She had a withdrawn intellectual aura, ragged clothing, and brush-lonely hair. Her skin was white. Pure white. White face. White neck. White hands. White enough to be dead. Not surprising though.

She *was* dead.

She'd turned into stone, white stone. Her hair, eyelashes and nails seemed normal. He ran is fingers over her forehead-smooth stone. He knocked lightly on her forehead-hard white stone. People strolled by on the other side of the floor-to-ceiling windows peering curiously at the guy with the shoulder length tangerine hair and Hawaiian hula hula shirt knocking on the overly white woman's head.

"She was a regular," said the short good-looking woman standing beside him. "She was here every night." Her name was Julie-not the stiff, the good-looking woman. She was the owner of the Tenth Cup. Brunette hair flowed over her shoulders, stopping just short of some interesting cleavage. She noticed Boston noticing the cleavage and smiled. "Her name was Brandy. She was a librarian."

Librarian, thought Boston. *That would explain the print book.*

"She didn't speak much, just drank coffee and read a different book every day." She put a sympathetic hand on Brandy's shoulder. "We found her like this an hour ago. One of the coffee consultants noticed that she wasn't turning pages." Julie gave her a wistful look. "She read quickly. She did a lot of page-turning."

6

"But not anymore, I guess," said Boston with what he hoped was the appropriate amount of inflected regret. He was sure that Brandy had been a good person, coffee addiction, print books, tattered clothing and all. "Did she have any enemies?"

A spark of suspicion ignited for an instant in Julie's brown eyes and Boston felt her mood chill a degree or two. He had that effect on people. "Just a standard question. I have to ask it."

The chill ducked into a warm place, the smile was back full-faced. "Of course. It's just, you know, strange... finding a regular customer suddenly turned to stone for no obvious reason. Do you think it was deliberate?"

"I've never heard of anyone turning to stone before. It's too early to even make a guess."

Julie looked at Brandy sadly. "We're going to miss her around here."

Two women sitting at the table directly behind Brandy's seemed to be frowning pointedly in Brandy's direction. *Was that animosity in their eyes?* "Did you ever notice anyone giving her a hard time, any arguments?"

She pursed her lips, squinted her eyes, trying to remember. "No... no. She was a loner. Kept to herself. When she was here, she drank coffee and read books. She never actually talked to anybody except the coffee consultants and me. I can't think of anyone doing something like this on purpose." She ran her hand across Brandy's cheek. "I can't imagine anyone doing *this*, period." She looked over at the counter where a dozen people had materialized out of nowhere. She turned back to Boston, put a hand on his arm, smiling, big brown eyes professional but playful. "I really should get back with the girls. This is one of our busy periods."

Boston smiled and nodded and scoped out her ass as she walked back to the counter. *Nice sway.*

A silver ID bracelet dangled on Brandy's wrist. He took out his wallet, opened it and tapped it against the bracelet. The screen in his wallet brought up her picture and ID. Brandy Williams. Born April 7, 2034. Occupation: Librarian. That was all. No address. No phone. No email. He snapped a picture of her with his wallet and looked around. No one seemed to be watching him.

It was time. The vibrations surrounding Brandy had a story to tell. That was their way. Everything was vibrations and when vibrations came into contact with each other, they left an indelible impression, a story that could be read of past events if you just opened yourself to their tale. He closed his eyes and relaxed his shoulders. He let his awareness sink slowly into his tan dien, the center of his psychic gravity. He slowed his breathing, letting the air glide through his nostrils and into his lungs, visualizing the energy of the universe flowing in through his head, down through his chest and deep into his stomach. He let the air drift up into his throat and seep out of his mouth as the energy of the earth flowed up his legs and into his stomach. After three breaths, he was in the zone, charged with energy and relaxed. He listened with his inner ear, waiting for the vibrations to speak to him about Brandy.

As usual, the vibrations said nothing. Somebody else did the talking.

"She was a pain in the ass." Surfacing back into the world, Boston focused his eyes on a woman with blond-streaked brunette hair with bouncy curls cascading down to her shoulders. Wide, dark-rimmed glasses gave her an air of smart and sharp. She was a knockout. "She was disruptive," she said with a sonorous voice that might carry to the ends of a large room without jarring a single eardrum. "She got into her books and forgot where she was, reading out loud half the time, and I mean *out loud*."

"Sometimes she'd yell," said the woman sitting across from her, another beauty with pitch black hair and matching eyes and skin lustrously pale, like something caressed by the moon. "I mean, she'd be reading, lip-mouthing with a low rumble, and then she'd suddenly yell 'NO! YOU DAMN FOOL!' She made me pour half a cup of coffee into my lap one night."

"She told my date and I to keep the noise down once," said the brunette. "And then she went into a yelling rage a few minutes later over some bim in one of her books opening the wrong door. She might not have any enemies here, but she sure doesn't have any friends."

Boston looked back at Brandy. She looked intense, but not frenetic. But then, people who read print books were a strange breed, throwbacks to an age when people expanded their libraries with shelves instead of memory, an age when you couldn't set your book to read out loud or change the end of the story to one you liked. Looking back at the brunette, he said, "Did anyone ever raise their voices at her? Tell her to keep it down? Throw heavy objects at her head?"

They both nodded no, looking at each other to confirm their nods, punctuating them with tight lips. "I think most people were a little afraid of her," said the woman with the moon tan. "I mean, she might blow a fuse and go ballistic." She turned around and looked at Brandy like something you might step over on a sidewalk. "She was probably harmless, but she was big. I wouldn't want to have someone like her coming at me hopped up on pumped caffeine and attitude."

Boston looked back at Brandy and nodded. Pumped caffeine. One of the marvels of 21st Century genetics. Caffeine with ten times the potency of the natural stuff. Java that could make you walk on ceilings. Your body had to adjust gradually to the strongest blends. Newbies sometimes went into cardiac arrest. Brandy on pumped caffeine would have been two hundred pounds of high volume fury if she'd lost it.

"Could you let me know if you think of anything else," he said, extending his wallet toward the women. The brunette tapped the bracelet on her right wrist against his wallet. "My name is Boston Jonson. I'm the consultative investigator assigned to this incident."

The women giggled. "We know," said the brunette. "You're, like, in the webloids."

"All the time," said the moon tan.

"Any chance of intros to any of those thirty naked pagan women from the Kilburn Blind Man case?"

Damn, thought Boston. *Lesbians*.

His wallet buzzed. He snapped it open. It was Laurel from CI Central. "Laurel, I just got here. I haven't had a chance to get into trouble yet."

"You're trouble the moment you arrive on the scene." She said it jokingly. She liked him even though he was the biggest pain in the ass in her life. "Have you been over to eReads yet?"

"Stopped off for some Brandy first."

"Brandy? You're drinking on the job? Boston...
"

"The name of the dead woman."

"She's dead?"

"Stone cold."

"Same as the ones at eReads. Any ideas?"

"Not yet. Whatever turned her into stone did it fast, froze her into reading stance."

"Reading stance?"

"Print book reader."

"A Gutensaur." Laurel gagged a snarky laugh and forced the grin off her face. "Sorry."

Boston smiled. He liked Laurel. "So what's with eReads? I thought you sent someone in for a referral already."

"New guy. Thinks he's you. Even wears one of those outrageous hula hula shirts and dyed his hair orange. He recommended conflict resolution because they were in an argument when they suddenly turned into stone. We're sending him to a reality consultant."

"Reality's overrated."

"Well, here's a shot of overrated reality for you. Central wants... "

"Quick and dirty. Who's on my ass this time?"

"No idea yet. Somebody big."

"As usual."

"Check out the bodies at eReads. Maybe refer for an autopsy?"

Staring at Brandy's cheeks, he said, "I think we'd need a geologist for this autopsy. Here... " He pressed his wallet against her forehead and returned to Laurel. "Just sent you a spectrum. See if the boys can figure out what kind of rock she is. I'll get over to eReads now."

The woman in Boston's wallet smiled. "Just keep it simple and make a referral, Boston."

"What I always try to do, Laurel." He snapped his wallet shut just as a frown began to spread over Laurel's mouth. He winked at the two beauties. "Thanks again for your help, ladies." They nodded and smiled as Boston walked to the counter and signaled to Julie who was making an elaborate coffee concoction that seemed more whipped cream and spices than coffee. "I need the body to be undisturbed while I check on something. I'll be back in about an hour. Do you mind leaving her be for the time being?"

Julie gave Brandy a sympathetic look and turned back to Boston with a smile. "That's OK, Mr. Jonson." She winked. "I think she's earned a little breathing space before she leaves for the last time."

Chapter 2

eReads was across the street and half a block down from the Tenth Cup, an easy walk. Except for the Magcab that tried to kill him as he stepped into the street. Running on magnets made them spooky quiet, and they moved fast. A gorgeous blond in the back seat waved and winked at him as the cab sped by. Boston Jonson might have been a trouble maker, but he was a famous trouble maker-the Creme de la Crop of the CI fold, society's filter between crime and the cops. They sent him in to, first, determine if an actual crime had been committed, in which case he dumped it into the cops' laps, or second, determine if something else had been committed and then refer it to whomever: social workers, gurus, reality reconstructivists. Every incident started with pieces scattered over the jigsaw puzzle they called the scene. Boston was the one who figured out how the first few pieces fit together.

But he liked jigsaw puzzles and sometimes he went too far. Pushing open the door to eReads, he read the sign taped to it:

No PRINT Books Allowed

eReaders Only

An angry red line slashed through an icon of an open print book. Boston wondered if that was some kind of censorship, but looking over the crowd, he noticed that everyone had holotops and an array of other electronic reading devices. This was a serious eCrowd, almost religious in their purism. Stands and shelves lined the walls displaying covers of ebooks, ezines, interactive webloids, and other electronic reading material. Everything on the shelves could be bought only through touch screen menus built into the covers. *Looks like you can still judge a book by its cover*. There were about twenty packed tables at the front of the shop, another twenty or so on a raised floor with a black metal railing surrounding it. Boston saw them immediately.

Strangely, he seemed to be the only person who noticed something odd. People walking by the two men frozen stone cold in the middle of what appeared to be a heated argument didn't even spare them a curious glance. He went to the counter and asked a crew cut man in jeans and untucked dirty shirt for the manager. He *was* the manager. His name was Earl. "We noticed them about an hour before closing yesterday." He gave the two men a distant look. "They're usually not this quiet." He came around the counter and walked over to their table with Boston.

They were frozen in stone just like Brandy, their eyes intent on each other, mouths open, talking at the same time-a heated discussion judging from the angry furrows over their eyes. One of them wore running gear-expensive terrain-adjusting nano shoes, skintight all-weather slacks, and what looked like one of the new nano massage sports coats. *Definitely not a poor man*. The other was dressed the exact opposite-torn running shoes with untied laces, army surplus pants and filthy t-shirt.

This pair didn't make any sense to Boston, but then, he wasn't into the coffee shop world, preferring restaurants and bars. Mostly bars. "Were they regulars?"

"Every day. They rarely came in together, but they'd always arrive within a few minutes of each other. They were addicts."

"Addicts." Boston curled his lower lip in disgust. He'd read about some of the new coffee blends that had been genetically engineered to be as addictive as heroin.

"Into the super caffeine blends. Stuff has to be served by specialized coffee consultants. You need a prescription to buy it."

This was new information to Boston. "A prescription to buy coffee?"

Earl nodded. He had a friendly glint in his eyes and a sort of puppy dog face, lab-like. "It's not unusual for coffee consultants to have backgrounds in pharmacology or chemistry. They have be qualified to fill prescriptions for these blends."

"And they're legal." The lip curled tighter.

"They're coffee." That seemed to say it all for Earl. Boston let it drop. The legalization of pot had done interesting things to social attitudes.

Boston and Earl walked up three steps and over to the table where the two men sat eerily lifelike, but so white.

"Well-dressed one is Bob," said Earl. "The other guy is Rob. You can smell his BO a mile away." Boston could smell it on his clothing a few feet away.

16

"They seem to have been arguing." Boston tapped Rob lightly on the forehead and heard the same muted thunk that Brandy's forehead had produced. Earl eyed him disapprovingly.

"That was what they did," said Earl. "They drank coffee and argued, you know, about philosophy, economics, religion, movies."

"Did they ever get violent?"

Earl laughed. "Not these two. They did things with words, not actions. They wouldn't even bang their fists on the table. Raised their voices when they wanted to make a point."

"Did they raise their voices much?"

"They had a lot of points to make."

In spite of the smell coming from Rob, Boston moved in for a closer look. Both men had their hands wrapped tightly around their cups, large white cups with no decals. They were bent forward, almost in each other's faces. "Did they have any enemies?"

Earl thought for a moment and shook his head slowly. "Not that I know of. They could get a little loud sometimes, but most of us just drowned them out. Sometimes people would use earphones, listen to music."

"No one ever threatened them?"

"Good god no. No threats. They weren't *that* loud." He looked around the coffee shop. "I'll admit, we have some strange people come through here. That's just the nature of coffee shops. Like I said, some of the hybrid brews are powerful, but these two could handle it. If not, the consultants wouldn't fill their prescription."

"So they were arguing one moment, and the next, they were stone. How long were they like this before somebody noticed them?"

Earl's voice took a defensive turn. "Well... we're not really sure. They were here for a couple of hours, not as loud as usual, so they weren't attracting as much attention as they might, and it was busy. One of the coffee consultants noticed them about an hour before closing. The place was packed and we were running out of cups. She went over to see if they were finished with theirs and became suspicious when she noticed they were just staring at each other and saying nothing. We also had the ambient music pumped a little louder than normal last night."

Boston noticed music playing in the background. Post Digital Death Punk. Loud stuff, but the volume was turned down to an ungentle murmur, what Earl meant by ambient. He leaned in closer to the two men, studying their faces. Not a sign of anything going wrong with their bodies. No raised eyebrows for a sudden realization like, "Hey, I think I'm turning into stone!" They were two men arguing about the ontological proof for the existence of God or the merits of Karaoke one moment, ornaments the next. Same as Brandy. Whatever happened to these people happened fast. They didn't know what hit them.

Earl shuffled up beside him, bent his head almost to Boston's level. He spoke secretively and seemed slightly embarrassed. "You know, you can't get anything like this in any of the catalogues."

Boston squinted his eyes, puzzled. "What are you talking about, Earl?"

"You know." He pointed a thumb at the two men. "They're the perfect coffee shop decor, life-size statues of coffee shop mood."

"Your point being?"

"Well, when you contact their families... " Now he was blushing. "Well, you know, maybe you could get them to contact me. I could make them an offer."

"An offer?"

"To buy the bodies. I mean, they're stone. They're not going to fit into any casket I've ever seen. They can't cremate them. What are they going to do... put them on the front lawn? I could make them a great offer. Keep them here. Maybe even put a commemoration plaque on their table."

That was enough for Boston. He smiled and nodded. Earl smiled and nodded and said, "I see this as win-win for everybody, including these two. I mean, they practically lived here. All you have to do is just mention it to their families."

"OK, Earl, I'll do that."

As Earl returned to the counter, Boston ran his wallet over Bob's ID ring-it was studded with what looked like real diamonds. Big diamonds. Robert Howard. No phone. No email. No address. Just Robert Howard. Boston sometimes wondered about the whole ID thing. On the other hand, it might have been full of information if Robert Howard wanted to release it to a lovely young lady, but he didn't think that he would be doing much of that with his coffee addiction and arguments with Rob.

19

Rob had no obvious ID tags. Boston felt his pockets. No wallet. Just Rob. *Guess his BO was his ID*. He took pictures of both men.

It was time to explore the vibrations. Two lives simultaneously flicking out-there had to be something floating in the air. He closed his eyes and slowed his breathing, letting the chi in the air and ground flow through his body. He sunk into a deep state of relaxation with each inhalation, letting tension out with each exhalation. His awareness wafted down like a leaf falling out of a tree to settle behind his belly button. He suspended all conscious thought and focused on the emptiness of his mind, a huge expanse of awareness containing nothing but the frequencies of the absent thought. He was a vibration fork ready to knock against the reality of the two dead men and play their story. Yes, he could feel the impact. On his arm.

Someone knocked lightly on his arm a second time. It was a middle-aged woman wearing narrow glasses over dilated eyes. She had tightly curled short hair, giving her stark face a sense of desperate panic. Sitting across from her was a man who could have been her twin, except his hair was longer and he was wearing a faded three-piece suit. The woman wore a plain brown dress that could have passed for an expensive potato sack.

"The world is a much better place," she said in a sincere voice, nodding her head in agreement with herself. The man nodded as well.

"And why do you think that?" said Boston.

"They were two very unhappy men." The man nodded agreement. "Their time was wasted, day after day, coming in here and arguing about nothing. They never even listened to each other, just talked at the same time." The man nodded. "The only thing coherent that ever came out of those two was that they argued about the same thing-they stayed on topic."

"I'm not sure that I'm getting this." Boston stepped closer to their table. Something assailed his nose. Was it the woman's perfume? The man's aftershave?

The woman took a big swig from her oversized cup, swallowed loudly and turned back to Boston. She looked almost panicky, but she spoke slowly, quietly, conspiratorially.

"Each night they picked a topic and then they talked. They never heard a thing the other said. They just sat there, face-to-face, talking *at* each other, like they saw each other as targets to throw words at." The man looked at her and nodded, looked at Boston and nodded. The woman nodded at Boston. Just for the hell of it, Boston nodded. "My brother and I... " She pointed at the man in the faded suit. "... noticed this almost as soon as they started coming here a few months ago. They were very loud when they got into it, like they were trying to drown each other's words with the loudness of their own words, win the argument by volume."

"And they never made any threatening moves toward each other, bang their fists on the table, throw coffee in each other's faces?"

The woman's laugh smacked of turbo-boosted caffeine. "The coffee those two drank is like gold. You don't waste a drop of it."

"Did anyone else ever threaten them? Throw cheap coffee in their faces?"

"Nobody wastes coffee around here. Even if anyone did tell them to keep it down, I doubt if it would have done any good. Those two heard everybody else about as much as they heard each other." Her brother nodded. "And Rob, the one who never tied his shoe laces... well... to put it mildly, he smelled... strong."

"I noticed that." *And either you or your brother, or both of you, smell even stronger.* "Did the management ever have to tell them to keep it down?"

"You don't do that in a coffee shop, Mr. Jonson. That could be suicidal. Coffee and the people who drink it are not things to be tampered with." She seemed almost proud to say this.

"You know who I am?" Boston was beginning to warm up to her.

Both the woman and her brother laughed nervously. "Of course we do. You're in all the webloids. The Kilburn Blind Man case was the greatest referral ever made. Although, you really didn't get around to referring until there was nothing left to refer." She and her brother snickered. "Thirty naked pagan women. How did you get them to do it?"

"Trade secret."

The woman frowned. *Another lost fan?* He was used to it. "Maybe I could give you their number?"

She beamed. He nodded. Things were copasetic. His wallet buzzed. It was Laurel.

"Just got word of another one," she said.

"Looks like coffee's getting to be a dangerous thing around here."

"Coffee's been dangerous for years now, Boston."

She paused.

"Laurel, you just paused. Something's up."

"Pressure from upstairs is building. The president of the Coffee Consultants and Coffee Shop Union is pulling strings all around us on this one. She's building a case that there might be a major coffee crisis, people being scared away from the coffee shops, going to bars instead. She's building a case around intellectual levels dropping all around the city as people drink more booze and less coffee, people being pulled over on sidewalks for drunken walking. The city is worried that they won't be able to drum up enough community work for them."

"Laurel."

"Yes Boston."

"That's the most ridiculous thing I've ever heard."

"This woman is connected internationally-coffee cartels, politicians, distribution unions. She's powerful. She's heard about you. She doesn't like you. She thinks you're trouble."

"I am trouble."

Laurel frowned. "This woman can hurt you."

"And how does that make this case different from any others?"

"Boston. It's not a case, it's a referral. It's a case when the police get your referral."

"You said there was another one."

"Just around the corner from where you are."

"Seems to be confined to this area."

"So?"

"Could be something in one of the coffee orders coming to this area. Or maybe someone operating locally."

"You think it might be deliberate?"

"So far, none of the dead people were well-liked."

"Meaning?"

"Someone may have had it in for them."

"Let the police make that determination, Boston. Just get your ass over to Lamb's Coffee House."

"Coffee *house*?"

"It's a coffee thing. The owner's waiting for you."

Chapter 3

Coffee House.

It was straight out of the 1950s-dark, moody, a place to stand up and read wild ranting poetry. A place to howl against the system. Three men with goatees and crew cuts sat in a cluster of armchairs surrounding a low wooden coffee table. They passed a joint around, hauling deeply, coughing. They could have stepped out of the Village at the height of the Beat Movement.

Large colorful abstract paintings blasted confused messages from the walls. A menu propped on an easel announced the day's special: smoke meat on rye with lentil soup and a beer. Clusters of armchair islands led up to a low stage with a microphone and stool. Nobody was howling angst today. There were just the three Beats and the back of someone's head sticking over the top of an armchair close to the stage. It was a still head with a white neck. The latest victim.

"Found him like that half an hour ago," said a harsh female voice to Boston's right. She stood behind a narrow cluttered counter. She was tall with unkempt white hair, dark horn-rimmed glasses and stark eyes. Her presence emanated the deeper meanings of dour. Boston had no idea what that meant, but it was how she made him feel. "My name is Lamb. This is my coffee house. I want that thing... " She pointed at the head. "... out of here as soon as possible."

"I'm... "

"I know who you are. Just get that thing out of here."

"Was he a regular?"

"He was."

"Was he irritating in any way?"

Lamb raised her eyebrows. The three Beats in the corner snickered and cackled. "He had a cell phone."

"Everybody has a cell phone."

"I don't."

Something in Lamb's severely simplistic look hinted at an invisible shield that would protect her against a hundred years of communications technologies.

"So his cell phone made him irritating?"

"His cell phone was an excuse for *him* to be a pain in the ass. Take away the phone and he'd find another way to be a pain in the ass."

"When did you notice something was wrong?"

"When he stopped being a pain in the ass."

"And just how was he being a pain in the ass?"

"Talking on that damn phone. Loud. Constant. He never shut up."

"And your customers noticed."

"A man talks non-stop on a cell phone with nobody in front of him to cushion the sound, it carries. But it wasn't just that." She put down a dish towel that she'd been kneading and leaned over the countertop. Boston almost stepped back.

"It was the way he talked. He talked low for a few minutes and then loud for maybe a minute and then low and then loud." A small deposit of white spittle appeared at the corner of her mouth. Her eyes grew menacing. "If he just talked loud or low, we could've tuned him out, chalk him off to background noise. But he talked low. We got used to it, not hear it. Then he suddenly raised his voice. It was like a slap in the ears. It was all you could be aware of. People lost their train of thought, forgot what they were talking about." Boston glanced at the three men smoking pot in the corner. *Not hard to see how that could happen.* "He had a deep voice. It carried like little waves of thunder."

"Is that why there's only a few people in here?"

Lamb's eyes narrowed. She wiped the spittle from her mouth with the back of her hand. "This is a licensed coffee house. We get a big crowd in here when the coffee shops close. They need the alcohol after a night of drinking coffee. We'll be packed tonight same as every night."

"Has there been anyone else in here besides the stiff, you and the three in the corner?"

"We had a poetry reading earlier. About two dozen people were here. He... " She nodded her head toward the body. "... talked on his phone through the whole thing."

"And you didn't ask him to keep it down or leave?"

"You don't do that to coffee drinkers. He was into the strong stuff. Prescription only."

"Did anyone go near his table?"

"Everyone was crowded around the stage area trying to hear the poets. Some people threw balled up paper at him. He ignored it. Kept talking."

"I'm going to look at the body. Do you know his name?"

"From the prescription... James something, but we call him Phone Dork."

"Cute."

He walked over to the body. It was the same as before. Whatever killed James Phone Dork took him quickly. No warnings, no symptoms, nothing alerted him to the fact that he was about to become a statue. He was frozen in mid-sentence, face blank, conversational, relaxed, just... talking on the phone. His mouth was still open. The black leather shoes, plain slacks and short-sleeved checked shirt suggested someone who probably didn't smoke pot or rant against the status quo. *What was he doing here*? He tried to pry the phone loose, but Phone Dork's hand was a stone container trapping it to his ear until somebody with a chisel broke it loose. He passed his wallet over the phone. No ID. He swiped it over his clothing. Nothing. He reached down and felt Phone Dork's back pants pocket and pulled out a wallet. It was the old type-no electronics.

Driver's license said he was James Cory. Twenty-six years old. He flipped through the card folder. *Interesting*. He was a nano-chemist, working for Chaney Pharmaceuticals. If Boston remembered correctly, they were one of the leading producers of genetically altered coffee beans, and rumored to be owned by entities in South America.

Time to see what the vibrations had to say. He lowered his shoulders, slowed his breathing, let his awareness sink, cleared his mind.

"Don't even think about trying that voodoo bullshit," called Lamb from the counter. "We don't do that weird religion stuff here."

28

Boston's wallet buzzed.

"Yes, Laurel."

"First, Brandy is stoned on calcium."

"Calcium?"

"It's actually a mineral. It's also what we would all turn into eventually if we were to live long enough. Second, the Friendliest Little Coffee Shop in the World. Two doors down from eReads."

"You want me to go there and make friends?" He tilted his wallet as he spoke and took a picture of Phone Dork.

"They have a statue they want removed."

"Busy murderer."

The face on the tiny screen frowned. "Boston! Murder is for the police to decide... *after* you've made your referral."

"The phenomenon seems to be moving faster than I can refer."

"Well you get to take a short break before you look at another body. Jane Wayne wants to see you. Pronto."

"Jane Wayne?"

"President of the Coffee Consultants and Coffee Shop Union. Her phone's been ringing off her wrist. She wants to know what the hell's going on."

"People starting to jump from coffee to beer already?"

"The moment the media gets onto this, there's going to be panic. A lot of people would like to see coffee come under stricter controls. This could be the ammo they need."

"Or maybe we need the stricter controls."

"That's not your call, Boston."

"Laurel, I need some info."

"Whatcha got?"

"James Cory. He's the stiff here at Lamb's. He was a nano-chemist for Chaney Pharmaceuticals. They're big in hybrid coffee's aren't they?"

"Check it out for you. In the meantime, Wayne's in the Carleton Building right around the corner from you."

"Handy."

"Just tell security who you are. She's expecting you. Five minutes ago. And be careful, Boston. This woman is powerful enough to shoot you on the spot, get a medal for it, and have your corpse doing a hundred hours of community work."

"I don't think my fans would like that."

"Your fans read the webloids. They'll just gobble it up, be mildly disturbed for fifteen seconds and read the next story."

"How ephemeral my fame."

"No, Boston. Not fame... notoriety. You're six minutes late. I'm smelling cordite."

Chapter 4

Carelton Place was the new breed of red brick building-nano bricks that would withstand most explosives short of a direct nuclear blast, mirror-surfaced airtight windows that would need a solar flare to heat them, and vidcams connected to every known terrorist, criminal, and crackpot in every police, military and community work facility in the world. Concealed laser sensors scanned anyone with a suspect ID. Carleton Place was a storage facility for important people.

It was where Jane Wayne waited for him and he was already twelve and a half minutes late. The security guards-avid followers of the webloids, recognized him immediately. They smiled and waved him through to the security elevator. Three seconds after the doors closed, they opened on the sixth floor. He hadn't felt a thing. *Smooth.*

He faced a long hall with no doors, windows or signs, except the one where Jane Wayne waited for him. The hall was lined with doors, but they would only appear to those with appointments. The sign beside the door read:

Coffee Consultants and Coffee Shop Union
Jane Wayne, Consulting President

The door slid open when he was six feet away from it. The office was huge with fifteen foot high ceilings, high corner windows, a teak oval meeting table with high-backed chairs on one side and cushioned chairs surrounding a glass coffee table on the other. In the center, with a panoramic view of the city in two directions, Jane Wayne sat behind her desk looking intensely important.

"You're thirteen minutes and forty-two seconds late." Her voice was eerily deep and commanding for a chubby-faced woman who couldn't have been more than four feet tall. She wore a monocle with a gold chain dipping over her navy blue business jacket and white shirt-open at the top, no tie. The computer built into her desktop flickered out leaving a spotless surface reflecting Jane Wayne. Elbows on her desk, she leaned forward and it seemed to Boston that the monocled eye looked deep into his being and didn't like what it saw. "I want this situation off the table yesterday. Large sums of money are involved. International trade is indicated. Key persons are concerned about prominent issues arising from the occurrences. You can go now."

That was easy.

Chapter 5

The Friendliest Little Coffee Shop in the World was likely one of the most uncomfortable places in the world-high tiny round tables barely big enough to hold a cup and a holotop, high tiny stools with back support right where it would do the most damage to the human back. It was a place that welcomed you long enough to slurp down your coffee, scarf your snack quickly, and leave. A cafeteria-style counter with slices of chocolate cheesecake and other foods guaranteed to dump five pounds on a paunch on first glance ran the length of one wall. The lighting was uncoffeeshopish bright for a clientele with dilated eyes. Every table held a holotop with a geek-like body bent into the information stupid highway. They were all breaking the law of slurp-your-coffee-and-get-the-hell-out.

He saw her right away. She looked mid-twenties, hair shaved to her scalp, tight black body suit, nose and ears and lips pierced and ringed. CyberGoth. Her holotop was one of the new ones that projected the keyboard onto the tabletop or into the air in front of her and projected the screen around her head for full immersion Net, all from a tiny crystal cylinder that she wore on a thick silver chain around her neck. Probably had sensory input/output as well. This woman had been in other worlds when she'd chalked it in.

"Get body out of here!" It was a shrill voice attached to a shrill woman, a tall shrill woman with high eyes, long wavy black hair, black slacks and sweater. "You Boston Jonson! You take body away!"

"Sorry, mam, but I just write 'em up. I don't do body removal."

Her eyes and nostrils flared. "You write up body to go away! Bad for business! She bad woman, noisy tap tap woman!"

He looked at the woman frozen in stone. Her hands hovered over the holo-projected keyboard on the tabletop. She could have adjusted it so that she would have been typing in the air, but some people preferred to feel their fingers actually touch something.

"She tap tap loud. Every day. Tap tap tap!"

"So she was a regular?"

"Always tap tap. Every day for over month."

"Did she have any enemies here?"

"Everybody hate her! Everybody want to put holoboard up her poop place."

"Did anybody actually talk to her, threaten her, throw tables at her?"

"She coffee drinker. Very strong coffee. Need prescription. Not good to mess with her."

"And your name is?"

"Linda May. Own shop. How long before body gone?"

"I can't really say, Miss May. But if everyone cooperates, it shouldn't be long. How long ago did you find her like this?"

"Half hour. Tap tap stop."

"Did you know her name?"

"Prescription say Thelma Rice. See? Cooperating. Get body out!" She turned quickly and

34

went back to the counter where two women in black robes and hoods waited to be served.

"She did it on purpose," said a short woman in an ankle-length black dress with a frilly neckline that plunged into two very large breasts. "She didn't have to type on the table."

"Some people prefer to have their fingers feel something."

"Feeling something is one thing. Pounding the life out of a tabletop with your fingers is another. When she was going full-tilt, you could see the surface of your coffee vibrating. Nobody types that hard, or that loud."

"Did you notice anyone going close to her around the time she stopped typing?"

"Nobody that I could see."

"Did she act strange today? Any change in her habits? "

"She came in, bought coffee, set up her holo and started pounding the shit out of the table."

"And nobody ever approached her about it?"

"Don't do the coffee shop thing much do you?"

"Guess not." He turned his head back to Thelma. The holo was still on. He thought about it a moment. *Should I?* It was tempting. Too tempting. He stepped in closer to Thelma's table, passed his head into the translucent circle of light around her head and entered the world that Thelma Rice had occupied when the tap tap had stopped.

The Free Coffee Coalition. Boston had heard of them. There were thousands of them spread around the world. They were mostly coffee swillers with a monstrous chip on their shoulders-they were addicts, addicted to coffee, and their lives as ruined as if they were hooked on heroin or alcohol. The cascading web pages showed pictures of Coalition members dressed in khaki creeping through the jungles of Columbia armed with guns and the incendiary devices they used to burn the crops of the coffee cartels. There were webloid articles with photos showing Coalition activists being executed by Columbian and Peruvian coffee farmers. One of the sites was a Coalition forum where the members went to mourn their fallen comrades, bitch about the cartels and encourage each other to vote against the politicians and bureaucrats at home who were on the cartels' payrolls to keep the coffee pouring.

Thelma was in the process of making an interesting entry in the forum.

Dannyg did it! It works! He made it! It really works! Soon... very soon, we'll all have the good stuff... and give it to the wor

And that was all she wrote.

Looks like Thelma and Dannyg were onto something, thought Boston. *The good stuff. And they were going to give it to... the wor? The world?* But unless Dannyg was still around, whatever the good stuff was, no one would be getting it. And what exactly was the good stuff? Judging from the sites, probably coffee.

And who was Dannyg?

Chapter 6

The Tenth Cup was packed. The two lesbians were gone. Conversation buzzed in the air. The smell of fresh roasted coffee was thick and creamy. Brandy was still white, still dead, and still pretty much ignored by the other customers. Julie smiled at him as she left the counter and walked towards him. The smile was a front, something for the customers, straight PR. When she reached him at Brandy's table, the smile evaporated into the coffee-drenched air, replaced with pursed lips over worried eyes.

"Word's been going around from the other shops." Small lines in the corners of her eyes would have added years to any other woman. Attached to Julie's eyes, they added character without the years. "It seems like there's some kind of epidemic going around?"

Boston smiled. "I don't think it's anything contagious."

"Do you think it's deliberate?"

"I can't be sure yet, but a few pieces are fitting together. Did Brandy's coffee need a prescription?"

"You think it was the coffee?" The lips tightened. The lines around the eyes looked less flattering.

Boston put a hand on her shoulder. "No. It's in a few places and only one in each... two in one of them. If something were wrong with the coffee, there'd be hundreds of statues in coffee shops around the city."

This seemed to reassure her. "Then... ?"

"Don't know what it is, but I'm sure it's not the coffee. Did hers... " He nodded toward Brandy. "... need a prescription?"

Julie crossed her arms, propping up the cleavage. Boston fought a close battle with his eyes. "Normally, yes." She raised an arm and pinched her lower lip. "But not today."

"Not today? You're sure?"

"It took us all by surprise. She ordered one of the flavoreds. Honey Almond Espresso, I think."

"And it doesn't need a prescription?"

"It's just normal coffee. Nothing like the Columbian Red."

"Columbian Red?"

The shake from Julie's giggle traveled nicely over the cleavage, but Boston only noticed this through peripheral vision. He was still waging war with his eyes. "You really don't know your coffee do you?"

"Educate me."

She smiled mischievously. "It's the most potent of all the coffees from Columbia. They named it after a particularly strong variety of marijuana popular in the 1980s. It's also the most addictive of all the coffees in the world."

"And it's legal."

"It's coffee."

"But Brandy wasn't drinking it today? Doesn't that seem strange? I mean, would the Honey Almond satisfy her addiction?"

"Not nearly-especially in here, around all this coffee. She should have been shaking and sweating within minutes. Withdrawal from Columbian Red can be dangerous."

Boston looked at Brandy. He looked at the tiny cup of coffee still pinched between the enormous thumb and finger. He took out his wallet and placed it over the cup. Julie looked at him curiously. "Taking a spectrum analysis for the lab boys."

"So you do think it was the coffee."

"Could be anything at this point, but I have to check out everything. Did she ever order other coffees in the past?"

"Not since the Columbian Red came out. It was all she would drink. They have a saying around it: Once you go Red, you stay till you're dead." She started to smile, but her eyes caught Brandy's white face and the smile quickly turned into a frown. "She had her ways, but she didn't deserve this." She looked back at the growing line-up at the counter and back to Boston. "I'd better get back to work." The smile was back. "I know that you might not be allowed, but if you could let me know what happened to Brandy when you find out, I'd be very grateful." She put her hand on Boston's arm and winked just before she left. Boston gave up the battle with his eyes and caught a quick glance of cleavage as she turned to go back to the counter. He caught the sway too. He loved his work. And speaking of work, he called Laurel.

"Boston, I think Jane Wayne is getting ready to put out a contract on you. Please tell me you're ready to make a referral," said the woman in his wallet.

"Getting there, Laurel. Nice to know you're worried about me."

"Your CI insurance pays out three times if you're murdered on the job."

"Anyone ever fake their murder?"

"Twice."

"And?"

"We made it official for them."

"You're joking."

"Of course I am." She didn't smile. "The referral?"

"Too early to know where to put this."

She frowned. He had that effect on people. "Why'd you call?"

"First, could you get the Boys to tap into Thelma Rice's holo. Look for any emails or other references to Dannyg."

"Dannyg? Who's he?"

"I don't know, but he's been up to something with Thelma. And here... " He pressed his wallet. "I'm sending you a spectrum of Brandy's coffee. It's supposed to be plain old Honey Almond, but she usually drinks Columbian Red."

"Columbian Red? I heard that once you go Red... "

"She's dead. But she was drinking something else. Let's see what the Boys can come up with. I also have a favor to ask."

"I'm already doing you a favor stalling Jane Wayne from making you the late Boston Jonson."

"Another favor. Could you call around to the other coffee shops, except Friendliest-I'm heading back there in a few-and find out what the other victims normally drank. And ask what they had for their last coffees."

"You think it was something in the coffee?"

"I'm not sure. Nobody else seems to be turning into stone, so it's isolated. They all had something in common-they were annoying people. But I don't think that had anything to do with their deaths. They were in coffee shops all around this area and I don't think anyone would have had the opportunity to put something in their java in the space of time they died."

"So?"

"So let's see what the Boys come up with. And let's see what they were drinking when they turned into stone."

"You're not thinking about solving this, are you, Boston?"

"Wouldn't dream of it. Just trying to figure out how to refer it."

"There's only one right way to refer this, Boston."

"How's that?"

"Fast."

He smiled and closed his wallet. He had a feeling that Thelma Rice was at the center of things.

Chapter 7

After almost being killed by another Magcab he walked into the Friendliest Little Coffee Shop in the World. Most of the same people he'd seen earlier were still there punishing their backs and seemingly unaware of it. Linda May was behind the counter serving coffee to a group of young people dressed in black loin cloths and so many metal piercings and chains that they clinked and rattled every time they breathed. As she passed a cup of coffee to a hand so heavily pierced that the fingers were almost invisible, she shrilled out, "You take tap tap woman away now!"

Boston nodded to her and strolled over to Thelma Rice's table. In spite of the piercings, and in spite of being bald and dead and having been turned into calcium, she was a beautiful woman with high cheek bones and almond eyes. Even devoid of color, her lips were full and sensual. *Dannyg was a lucky man-or had been a lucky man.* He wondered if Dannyg had any idea what had happened to Thelma.

He looked around. Nobody seemed to be looking at him or at Thelma. They were all wrapped in conversation, holotops and coffee highs. Perfect opportunity to delve into the vibes and get into Themla's head in those moments before her death. He crouched down beside her, slowed his breathing and began the process of centering his awareness.

"You take tap tap woman away!" It was somewhere between a loud command and a shriek. It almost hurt his eardrum. Linda May was crouched down beside him, her mouth less than a foot away from his ear.

Boston turned slowly to face her. As much as he wanted to strangle any throat capable of making an ungodly sound like that, he kept his voice low, patient. "That's not really my job, Miss May."

"She scare away customers! Take up space!"

Boston gave her his best pasted-on smile and looked around the crowded coffee shop as he spoke. "I don't think she's scaring anybody. I don't think anybody in here even knows she's dead. I don't think anybody in here even cares if she's dead. Could you back away a few feet and keep your voice down?"

Linda May clamped her mouth tightly and stared at him disbelieving. She stood up and stepped back. "Tap tap woman not stay here." It was just a few decibels short of shrill, but it was an improvement. His ear still ached.

"Tap tap woman stay right where she is until I make a referral and that will take a lot less time if I get fewer eviction orders and more cooperation."

Linda May glared at him.

"That's better. What kind of coffee did she usually drink?"

"She drink strong stuff, Columbian Red. Once you go Red... "

"I know, I know. But what did she drink today?"

Linda May's eyebrows raised. "No Columbian Red today. Just normal house blend. She still tap tap. Loud tap tap."

"And she never ordered the house blend at other times?"

"Columbian Red only. She addict. Have prescription."

"Did you notice if anyone went near her? Did she leave her table, go to the washroom-leave her coffee on the table while she was gone?"

"Nobody go near her. She never leave table, just sit and tap tap."

"Thank you. You can go back to work now."

Linda May stared at Boston, only half believing that he had just given her an order... in her own place. She huffed just barely enough for it to be visible and stalked back to the counter.

Boston considered tapping into the vibrations, but the mood had passed. His mind was suddenly cluttered with details. Both Thelma and Brandy were Columbian Red addicts. It was all either of them drank. But today, they drank an innocuous coffee that should have bounced off their coffee-hardened hides and then both had died. His wallet buzzed. It was Laurel.

"Looks like your hunch paid off, Boston."

"Columbian Red?"

"Every one of them. Hooked almost from day one when the stuff was first released."

"But not today."

"Not today. They all had ordinary coffee."

Boston perked up. "Non-prescription stuff?"

"Just plain old coffee. The Boys are going to do a nano-scan, see if that picks anything up. If they don't pick anything up, will you still have enough for your referral?"

"Let's see what the Boys come up with." Studying Brandy's features closely, he closed his wallet, wondering how a librarian fit into this. Maybe it was time to go to the library for some information.

Chapter 8

The library was two blocks away. Boston used the crosswalks, but was still almost run down by a Magcab making a right turn on a red light. He wondered if they won points for killing pedestrians.

The glass doors of the library scanned him as he entered and a digiboard implanted in the second set of doors greeted him in big red letters:

Welcome Boston Johnston.
Possibly these new titles will interest you:

It listed five books that Boston would never dream of reading. Not surprising-it couldn't even get his name right. He looked around, computer terminals everywhere, a few rooms for holotops, no shelves bursting with books. The real books were in the basement archives-their text digitized and displayed in the library or downloaded to personal devices. No humans in sight-employees or patrons. A wide stairway led up to the second level. He climbed the stairs up to a surprisingly quiet area given the number of people. The place was packed. As he was beginning to wonder what the attraction was, he noticed the coffee kiosk. They served coffee.

He crossed a shiny tile floor to the reception desk and a librarian with long grayish brown hair flowing over her shoulders. Rimless glasses covered most of the top half of her head. She pushed her head towards him as he approached her desk. "Can I help you?" It wasn't so much a question as it was an order to surrender information.

"Brandy Williams worked here?"

"Yes, and she's late."

"She won't be coming in today."

"And who are you?"

"Boston Jonson, CI." This seemed to have no effect on the big-glassed women. "I'm the consultative investigator working on Ms Williams death."

"She's dead?"

"It happened a few hours ago."

"How?"

"We're not sure yet. Where did Ms Williams work?"

"She worked here, in the library."

"Whereabouts in the library did she work? Her desk?"

She pointed to a raised section of the room. Boston looked around. From where Brandy sat, she could monitor the entire floor, all the holos, the coffee kiosk, everybody who came and went. He had a hunch that Brandy's vantage point in the library was what connected her to her death. And somehow to the deaths of the others. But how?

He walked over to the raised floor and stepped up to Brandy's desk.

"You can't do that," called the librarian at the reception desk. She seemed more curious than angry or authoritarian. Boston took out his wallet and his ID holo popped out the top. He expanded it so that the woman could read it. She huffed and went back to work.

Boston walked around the desk and sat in Brandy's chair. The holo was implanted in her desk lamp. He turned the lamp on. Brandy's connection displayed on her desktop. It was mostly archive information, library database stuff. There was a row of icons on the right side of the interface-mostly the standard stuff like programs for word processing, database management, media players... and one that he'd never seen before. It looked like a pair of eye glasses. He touched it lightly with his index finger. A password box appeared. He tried a few things. BrandyWilliams. Nope. Brandy. Nope. ColumbianRed. A new dialogue box appeared.

Security Action 3434-aa343

ADMIN RESET

*What the hell does that mean?*Obviously, he wasn't going to be getting into the eye glasses today. He took out his wallet, took a picture of the dialogue box and called Laurel.

"Boston! Jane Wayne just called. She wants your referral on her desk five minutes ago."

"On her desk? I work for Jane Wayne now?"

"HQ promised to forward it to her the moment they receive it."

"HQ works for her?"

"HQ is being hammered by the heat she's bringing down on them. They may shoot you before she does."

"They'll have to draw straws to see who gets to pull the trigger first. I'm not ready yet." He pressed on his wallet. "I'm sending you a message from a computer at the library... "

"Which one?"

"The one where Brandy Williams worked. The City Library."

"Whatcha got?"

"Tried to get into her work computer."

"It was pass protected?"

"You got it."

"It gave you three tries before it shut down?"

"So, you have cameras hidden in here?"

"We don't need them. The Boys will be inside the library network in minutes. Anything she has on her machine will be ours."

"How about Thelma's holo?"

"She was into the whole coffee freedom thing, on a few forums, mostly ranting about the Columbians and the coffee cartels. Nothing about Dannyg except some crazy thing about him doing it and soon they'll all have the good stuff and give it to, we think, the world. We know her whole life but there was nothing there about Dannyg."

"I like the way you said that. Gives me chills. You never let them tap into my wallet do you?"

"We own that wallet, Boston. We know more about it than you do."

"Well, that's really creepy. They come up with anything about the coffee yet? From the nano-scan?"

"Nano-scans take time. I don't think you have that long to live. Might have to make your referral without it."

"Another remark like that and I'll refer it to the National Geological Survey."

Laurel smiled and looked almost relieved. "Boston, I think that's a great... "

He closed his wallet. It buzzed. He opened it. Jane Wayne's monocled face filled the tiny screen. She didn't look happy.

"You're late. Information flow is converging on inappropriate points of focus. Financial correlations have been identified on possible market inefficiencies. Remedial action may be warranted. Is your referral ready?"

"Soon."

"Sooner."

The screen went blank. *Always nice talking to you*.

Chapter 9

Time to start pushing things. He smiled mischievously as he walked through the wood and brass doors of Chaney Pharmaceuticals. It was just a few blocks away from the library, and the toes in his right foot were sore from kicking the passenger side door of a Magcab that tried to kill him. Nearly two hundred years old, the Chaney building was a massive structure built with huge blocks of cut stone. Long ago, it housed government offices, but the government had long since moved out and moved into a vast network of online offices with civil servants who worked secretly in their basements and kitchens.

Chaney Pharmaceuticals used the building for public relations, which seemed fitting, given the huge chamber that Boston walked into. A giant crystal chandelier hung from the ceiling a good forty feet over a brilliantly polished marble floor. To his left, an arched doorway led into a coffee shop where regular blends were free but the good stuff sold at regular prices and required a prescription. Another arched door, to his right, led into a museum crammed with Columbian coffee lore-maps showing the grow areas, pictures of villages with smiling villagers in straw sombreros grasping plants brimming with coffee cherries. Framed documents told the story of Columbian coffee from the early days right up to the formidable brews in the late 21st Century. It looked like Chaney Pharmaceuticals was in the coffee business only, but Boston didn't bother with any of it. This part of the building was a whitewash for the public. What he was interested in was more likely in the maximum security facility that burrowed down over two hundred feet under the building. That's where the labs and research offices were located.

He looked around. Security in this area seemed light, with a few unarmed Columbian guards strolling leisurely or talking to visitors. They had wide smiles and great tans and spoke perfect English. He walked slowly up to an information desk where a beautiful Columbian woman with long jet black hair, sparkling white teeth and a brightly colored sundress sat. She smiled widely at him as he approached, big brown eyes beaming.

"Can I help you, sir." Even without the accent, her voice had a lilting South American flow.

He brought out his wallet and showed her his CI ID. "My name is Boston Jonson." He waited for the raised eyebrows of recognition. They never came. *Probably doesn't read the webloids.* "I'm working on a referral that involves one of your employees."

She just sat and smiled, waiting for him to continue.

"You have a nano-chemist named James Cory working here."

"Just a moment." She ran her fingers across the holoboard on her desk and read from a holoscreen located in the air between them, invisible from his side. She looked into Boston's eyes. "Mr. Cory no longer works here." She smiled.

"Would you mind if I ask why."

Her fingertips danced on the board again. "His contract expired. It wasn't renewed."

"And may I ask why?"

"I'm sorry, Mr. Jonson, but that information is very specific. You'll have to fill out an information request form and the information will be supplied to you within five working days."

He crossed his arms and rested them on the countertop and said in his best serious, but joking around voice, "You realize, of course, that refusal to cooperate with a CI referral is punishable by up to ten hours of community work."

"That much?" She feigned concern.

"We take these referrals seriously."

She handed him a form. "We take our confidential information seriously. You can have all the information you want by filling out the form, or... " She pointed to an island of holotopped information kiosks. "... you can fill it out electronically. It will still take five working days."

He took the form and stuffed it into his shirt pocket. "Thank you, mam."

She smiled.

He decided to leave it up to the Boys to crack into the Chaney database and get the information for him in five working minutes. As he walked toward the door, he noticed at least half a dozen security cams scanning him from head to foot.

That should get something moving.

Chapter 10

He wasn't out the door more than a second before his wallet buzzed. It was Jane Wayne.

"My patience is a dangerous flux."

The screen went blank.

His wallet buzzed again.

Laurel filled the screen.

He winked at her. "Is your patience turning into a dangerous flux as well?"

"Jane Wayne?"

"She's a woman of remarkably few words."

"She doesn't need words. She has the Columbians behind her. It's when she stops talking that you need to worry. Got some stuff for you."

"The coffee sample?"

"And Brandy's computer at the library."

"The Boys are fast."

"Seems that Brandy has been monitoring the library's clientele closely, especially two of them- Thelma Rice, codename ricecake, and Dannyg. They don't have a real name for him yet."

"I'm sure they will soon."

"They're working on it. They both have over a hundredf email accounts. The Boys are checking them out."

"And the coffee?"

"They're not sure yet. The nano-scan turned up some trace particles that don't fit the usual coffee profile, especially for normal coffee. But they could be anything. Was she wearing lipstick."

"She was all white."

"Her hair and nails as well?"

"Everything but her clothing and anything that wasn't part of her body."

"And her lips weren't red?"

"And just who's the CI on this referral?"

"So, she wasn't wearing lipstick. It could be anything though. They'll find out."

"What are the chances of the Boys getting into the Chaney systems?"

"They've been at it for years. Sometimes they get lucky, but Chaney is tight on security. They don't trust computers. Almost all their sensitive materials are delivered by runners."

"Bringing the jungle into the city?"

"It works. What are you looking for?"

"Apparently, James Cory doesn't work there anymore. His contract expired and wasn't renewed. The timing seems a little strange."

"Sounds like the kind of stuff that would be in their system. I'll get the Boys to look into it. By the way, Boston, have you ever met the Boys?"

"Can't say I have."

"Some of them really are boys, working in home labs that we set up for them, but mostly they're teenage girls, working out of their rec room and bedrooms. Some of them live in their pajamas. They work for us, play online games and read the webloids. They think you're just the greatest orange-haired hulu hulu shirt-wearing hunk in the world."

"And I respect them for that."

"Just think about that when they're monitoring your wallet."

Boston laughed. "My cyber chaperones."

"Boston." The smile dropped from her face. "Get this referral done fast... or your cyber chaperones will shut you down for your own good...if Jane Wayne doesn't get the honor first."

"I think I'll pay a visit to Bob and Rob."

"What's with them?"

"Not a clue. Just a feeling."

"Get on it... while you can still feel." Her smile was playfully sardonic.

Chapter 11

He had to admit, Bob and Rob did make compelling coffee shop sculpture, though he and Earl seemed to be the only ones noticing. He reached them at exactly the same time as Earl, who had a few beads of sweat popping across his forehead. He leaned close to Boston, smiling nervously. "Well?"

"Well what, Earl?"

"Did you get a chance to talk to the families?"

"Not yet, I'm afraid. Contact with families and friends is off-limits until I've filed my referral."

"And... ?"

"That should be soon, I hope."

This seemed to reassure Earl, who smiled and shook his head vigorously. "It's the right thing, y'know. What they would want."

"I'm sure it is. I'll keep you informed."

"I appreciate this, Mr. Jonson." He looked at the two statures and shook his head. "A shame, though. All those animated arguments silenced forever. And my apologies."

Boston looked at him inquisitively.

"I received a call from CI Central about what they were drinking. A new coffee consultant filled their prescription. If I had known they were drinking normal coffee, I would have mentioned it. It doesn't make any sense. Columbian Red was all they ever drank."

"No problem." At least he didn't recite the 'once you go Red' jingle.

Earl went back to the counter. Post Digital Death Disco played quietly and angrily in the background as people crowded around their tables burying themselves in holotops or reading from a variety of readers. He wondered if the ones whose fingers swept madly over their projected keyboards were adding to the vast free libraries, online bookstores, blogs and social reading sites that defined the publishing world of the late 21st Century. He recalled reading an article by a book reviewer bemoaning the fact that people no longer referred to books as mysteries or romances anymore, using instead 'mystery content' or 'romantic content."

Oh well, time to tap into the vibrations. He closed his eyes, let his shoulders drop, took a deep breath through his nose and...

"They're dead, aren't they?"

He opened his eyes. The strange couple he'd talked to earlier had been replaced by a beautiful woman with long raven black hair wearing a jogging outfit and brilliant white running shoes. She had dark almond eyes and a flattering sprinkle of freckles. And a dynamite body. Boston was stuck for words. She noticed and smiled. She extended her hand. "I'm Shelley."

Boston took her hand. He was tempted to kiss it, fondle it, worship it, but shook it instead. "I'm... "

"Boston Jonson." She smiled even wider. "I read the webloids." She removed her hand from his and pointed at Bob and Rob. "I'm guessing those aren't just statures of those two-that's really them, and you're here to refer?"

There was something in her dark eyes that inspired visions of untamed mares roaming the ranges of pure desire. He felt almost intimidated. "Yes, mam... "

"Shelley. Call me Shelley."

He hoped that wasn't a blush he felt creeping up his face. "Shelly. Um... new shoes?" He pointed at the radiant white sneakers."

"Bought them a month ago."

"And you've been running in them?"

"Every day."

"They look like you bought them today."

"I run carefully."

He looked around the room, noting the coffee stains on the floor. "Isn't this a dangerous place to bring them?"

"They know me here. They touch my shoes, they die."

Something in her voice and the muscles rippling under the jogging gear convinced Boston that she wasn't joking. "Did you know Bob and Rob?"

"Dated Bob once. He cancelled the second date to come here and argue with Rob. And that was before the two of them got hooked on the Red. Didn't date him after that."

"He stood *you* up for an argument?"

"Just the once." There was finality in the smile that touched those full lips, and not a trace of regret over losing a date with Bob. "So what do you think happened to them?" she said.

Boston glanced at the two. "I don't know. I've never heard of people turning to stone before. How was your date with Bob?"

"Boring. He didn't stop talking all evening... about everything under the sun, from one topic to another. He took me home early. Said he had some work to do. I think he might have come here to argue with Rob."

Boston raised his orange eyebrows. "And you were going to go on a second date with him?"

"Don't know what I was thinking."

"What was the attraction about arguing with Rob?"

"Not a clue. Might have been platonically gay or something. But now... I guess they get to spend the rest of eternity in mid-argument. I think they'd like that. Just a second... " She took a cell phone out of her pants pocket. It was exactly the same kind that James Cory used. Looking at it, something buzzed in the back of Boston's mind. *What is that?*

And then it hit him. James Cory, Phone Dork. Who had he been talking to during all those long annoying conversations at Lamb's? Was it a woman, a close friend or relation, a telehooker?

His wallet buzzed. It was Laurel.

"Laurel... "

"Got something for you, Boston."

"Great, but... "

"Rob."

"What about him?"

"The Boys matched his photo. His full name is Robert Gibson."

She paused for effect. Must be something big.

60

"And?"

"He worked at Chaney Pharmaceuticals. He was in security. It was his job to receive packages from the runners, examine them, record them, distribute them. He had access to all the top secret stuff."

"Do you think he would have known James Cory?"

"Over a thousand people work there and they're not allowed to fraternize outside work hours. They might see each other in the halls day-after-day and still be strangers, but we don't think Robert Gibson and James Cory were strangers."

She paused again.

"Please, Laurel, don't do this to me."

Her smile was definitely sardonic. "The same doctor prescribed their coffee. About three months ago they had back-to-back appointments. They would have been in the waiting room at the same time. About an hour later, they both had their prescriptions filled at eReaders... at the same time. They both ordered Columbian Red."

"Pair of coffee addicts getting together, maybe exchanging... um... did you say 'worked'?"

"He was laid off the same day that James Cory's contract expired."

"So the folks at Chaney connected the dots between the two of them."

"Looks that way. Strange though... " She paused. "... this isn't the way Chaney Pharmaceuticals-given its owners-would normally handle something like this. The two of them should have just... disappeared."

"But they didn't. You're right, that is strange. Maybe they were under surveillance to find out what they were up to?"

"They would have tortured that out of them."

Boston felt the stirrings of a shudder. These were the same people that Jane Wayne could sic on him. And he'd just finished walking into their lair to stir things up. Maybe it was time to speed up this referral.

And then again, maybe not. "Got another one for the Boys."

"Whatcha got?"

"James Cory spent hours on his cell, day after day, irritating the daylights out of everybody at Lamb's. Think the Boys can find out who he was talking to?"

Laurel laughed. It was a deep laugh, unrefrained, almost wild. If he weren't so used to it, it would have chilled him. In a nice way. "This, they could do with their eyes shut."

He noticed that Shelley had just finished her call. "Gotta go now." He snapped his wallet shut and pocketed it.

"Couldn't help hearing you say something about an irritating guy with a cell phone at Lamb's."

"You knew him?"

"Heard him. I went to a reading there earlier. He talked on the phone all through it. Everybody wanted to kill him."

Boston smiled. "Maybe everybody got their wish."

Chapter 12

He had a date with Shelley. But that was for tomorrow. For now, he had a referral to complete. He was pretty certain that by now Jane Wayne wanted him dead. He had that effect on people. But he was also certain that Jane Wayne could and would do it.

He was sitting in one of his favorite bars. He had lots of favorite bars. He liked the atmosphere in this one. It was Irish, with a huge selection of Irish beers and whiskeys. He took a long slow swallow from a mug full of ice cold Guinness and felt energy of another sort coursing through his body. It felt good.

It was time to reflect, to gather his thoughts and see what he had. Definitely not enough for a referral. Well, *maybe* enough for a referral, but not enough that he was ready to make it. He wondered how much longer he had before Jane Wayne called in the Columbians and received a medal for offing him. He put the thought aside with another long swallow. It felt good to be out of the world of coffee. He couldn't understand the attraction when there was so much great beer to be had.

Oh well, back to gathering his thoughts.

What did he have? Time for a mental list:

1. Five (5) people were dead, turned to calcium.

2. In each case, it happened fast enough to freeze them in mid-whatever-they-were-doing.

3. All five (5) were addicted to Columbian Red coffee.

4. All five (5) were annoying people who were disliked by pretty much everyone they came into contact with.

5. They all (5) were drinking innocuous brands of coffee when they died.

6. One (1) of them, James Cory, was a nano-chemist working for the company (Chaney Pharmaceuticals) that produced Columbian Red.

7. Another, Robert Gibson, worked as a security consultant for the same company.

8. Both had recently had their employment terminated by the company.

9. They had the same doctor and had certainly met at a mutual appointment to have their prescriptions for Columbian Red renewed.

10. Both had had their prescriptions filled shortly after at the same coffee shop.

11. This was against company policy, warranting disappearance.

12. Neither had disappeared.

13. However, both had died within hours of each other.

14. One (1) of the victims, Brandy Williams was a librarian who had been keeping tabs on another of the victims, Thelma Rice (username ricecake), at the library.

15. She was also keeping tabs on someone named Dannyg (real name unknown).

16. Dannyg had come up with something that works and soon everybody in the world was going to have the good stuff.

17. Who the hell was Dannyg?

18. Scratch that. Not a fact.

19. James Cory was having mucho irritating conversations with someone as yet unknown.

20. Thelma Rice was very likely affiliated with an organization that wanted to thwart the coffee cartels.

21. Robert Gibson met regularly to argue with Robert Howard.

22. Seven Magcabs had tried to kill him on the city streets. In one day.

23. Scratch that last point. Irrelevant to the referral.

24. Jane Wayne, Consulting President of the Coffee Consultants and Coffee Shop Union was on his case to get his referral done fast. Par for the course.

25. Earl wanted to buy two dead statues from their families to keep in his coffee shop.

26. The vibrations had turned up zilch. As usual.

27. If we live long enough, we turn into calcium.

28. In none of the cases did anyone have a chance to lace the victims' coffee with something that would turn them into stone.

29. The nano-scan turned up trace particles of something uncoffelike in Brandy's coffee.

30. The Boys were mostly Girls. In pajamas.

And the mental list added up to one thing: Who the hell is Dannyg?

His wallet buzzed. It was Laurel.

"Got something for you."

"Dannyg?"

"Nope. Something better. The Boys have been having a heyday breaking into Chaney Pharmaceuticals. Guess what they came up with?"

"The Secret Formula for Columbian Red?"

Laurel's eyes widened in surprise, then narrowed suspiciously. "That was just a guess, wasn't it?"

"Judging from the look on your face, I'd guess it was close."

"It was. Columbian Red was developed right here in town-and in a few other places-but this was the main operation. They were afraid that if they did it all in Columbia, the other coffee cartels would catch on and find a way to get to the research, so they spread it to labs around the world-the biggest one being right here."

"Where James Cory and Robert Gibson worked."

"There's a connection, Boston."

"There certainly is, Laurel."

"Ready to make your referral?"

"Getting close."

"I hope you're right."

"Why's that?"

"The Boys came up with something else."

"And... ?"

"Your name came up on a memo sent out less than twenty minutes ago. It was in Spanish. Most of it was garbledegook. The last sentence was interesting. It was *Jonson: eliminar*. That's Spanish for eliminate."

"So, how long do I have?"

"See any suspicious looking Columbians with machetes around you right now?"

He looked around the bar. Mostly non-Columbian Irish-looking folks quietly drinking their Irish beer. A table with three Chinese women drinking Irish whiskey. No machetes. "Nope. Guess I get to stir the shit a while longer."

"This is no joke, Boston. These are not the kind of people who go to jail for breaking laws."

"Puts me in good company. Anything on James Cory's mysterious cell phone mate?"

"Give them time. Breaking into Chaney was a major operation."

"Thank them for me."

"They'll be... oh... just got something else. Seems there was nothing much on Thelma's holo. She used it for the usual coffee rebel stuff-socializing with those of like coffee rebel mind, ranting and raving on the usual anti-cartel sites. She used the library holos to hack into politicians' and coffee cartel files. Looks like she was good at it. And she has plenty of email and user accounts to cover her tracks. Could've made a fine addition to the Boys."

"Except she got stoned and missed it."

"Still listening to ancient rock, Boston?"

"Still the best rock, Laurel."

"She's hit on Chaney a few times, but more interesting... "

"Yes?"

"Dannyg. Seems he's been hitting on Chaney as well-one particular account."

"Let me guess... James Cory."

"Cigar time. He's been going into Cory's account, downloading lots of sensitive stuff, stuff that, if we have his work right, he shouldn't have had on his computer."

"Like... ?"

"Like the nano-processes for Columbian Red. He was working on nano-assisted emulsions and processes for the lesser brands."

"The less addicting ones?"

"Right."

"So how... ?" It was like a sudden jerk on his head, a strong jerk. "Robert Gibson. Gibson was feeding him information about Columbian Red."

"And it looks like the Columbians knew about it."

"But why just terminate their employment? Seems to me they'd just kill them, tie up the loose ends. Maintain their reputation."

"And therein lies the mystery. Why were they allowed to live so long?"

"Maybe to find out if anyone else was involved?"

"That's my guess. And that's probable cause for murder. Also, probable cause to make a referral to the police."

"Not yet."

"Boston... "

"Still one thing I'd like to nail-Dannyg."

"Curiosity can get you eliminar on this one, Boston."

"Eliminar is my middle name."

"Right after Trouble."

68

"Let me know when the Boys find out who Cory was calling. I have a feeling he might have known Dannyg."

"You'll be the first to know."

He closed his wallet and pocketed it, and wondered where he could stir up the maximum amount of the brown stuff and stay alive in the process. Lamb's?

Chapter 13

Amazingly, no Magcabs tried to kill him on his way to Lamb's, but he knew they were out there... waiting. The three Beat potheads were still in the corner, still passing a joint around, still giggling and talking quietly, still looking at Boston with glazed suspicious, half-amused eyes. There were a few people at other tables, sipping drinks, passing joints, none of them aware of the white head facing the stage. Lamb glared at him. "Coming to take the body away?"

"No, mam, just trying to get my referral done. Mind if I ask a few questions?"

"Will it take long?" Her expression was dead-pan. He wondered if she ever smiled. *Probably not.*

"A minute or two."

"Make it a minute." There was something about this cell-phoneless woman that unsettled Boston. He could get tough with her, but he wondered what Doors to Dour that would open. He decided he didn't want to know. "Can you remember the tone in James Cory's voice when he talked on his phone?"

"Tone?"

"Did he seem happy, sad, angry, romantic, reflective, grievous, joyful, sardonic, evil, exuberant, coy, frightened, threatening, business-like, friendly, carefree, tentative, awed, bored, excited, chastised, perturbed, enlightened, cuckolded, mystified, curious, befuddled?" He winked. "Tone."

Lamb stared at him as though he had just stepped off the elevator from Mars. There were better ways than waving the rules to get people to cooperate and Boston Jonson was good at all of them.

"Any of the above?"

She finally managed to move her lips and the flattest most deadpan voice he could imagine scraped off her tongue. "It went quiet, it went loud."

"And that's it?"

"That's it."

"Thank you." He strolled over to James Cory's petrified remains. The phone was still in his hand, but the Boys would be breaking into his service provider's files soon and tracing his calls. He didn't look like a nano-geek. He had a strong face, something you might picture on a firefighter or cop, maybe even a CI. Boston wondered if James Cory knew Dannyg. Were they in cahoots together to steal coffee secrets from Chaney Pharmaceuticals? He glanced quickly back at the counter where Lamb served some concoction in an over-sized cup to a man with a goatee and black beret, who looked like his shirt and pants might have been sitting around unwashed but thoroughly worn since the days of the Beat Movement.

Time to go for it. He emptied the air from his chest, pushing it out with just the slightest force from his stomach and breathed in through his nose, filling his chest, feeling the chi energy beginning to flow through his body like a wave of pure knowledge of the universe. His ears filled with a sound like currents swirling in the Knowingness of

All. And something else. He ducked his head to the left just in time to miss having half of it cleaved off by a machete spinning viciously through the air at him. It stuck itself deep into a wooden post behind the stage. Boston's head snapped toward the door just in time to see it closing.

Lamb and the Beat throwback stood with their eyes wide, looking first at Boston, then at the machete buried in the post and then at the door.

"Did you see who threw that?" He said it calmly, pointing a thumb at the machete. It wasn't the first time someone had tried to kill him. Lamb and her customer nodded no, eyes still wide.

His wallet buzzed. It was Laurel. She looked worried. "You all right, Boston? The Boys just cracked a message from Chaney about the Boston Problem being taken care of."

"The Problem's still here. They missed."

"Machete?"

"Sharp one."

"Ready to make your referral?"

"In spite of the Columbian pep talk, we'll see. Any word on James Cory's calls?"

"Not yet, but the Lab Boys... by the way, the Lab Boys are mostly male. They work onsite, in labs."

"Are they fans too?"

"They don't read the webloids. When they're not in the lab, they're spread across the world in games. They found something interesting in Brandy's coffee. Those particles turned out to be nano-trace."

"Nano-trace?"

"Worst kind. They're not sure yet, but it looks as though it may be assemblers."

"There were assembler nanobots in Brandy's coffee?"

"Like I said, they're not sure yet. It could be something else, but their first guess is assemblers."

"Damn." It was a quiet damn, something coming from a place of mild disappointment.

"What? This is good, Boston. This might give us some insight into how five people have been flash-frozen into calcium."

"It also means that somebody had to put the bots into their coffee, but nobody had a chance to do that."

"Coffee house staff? Stick a few bots in while pouring?"

"In all four places? Not likely. Besides, Lamb doesn't even have a cell phone. She sure as hell wouldn't have nanobots up her sleeve."

"Well, at least think about it, Boston. I mean, they were all very annoying people. The ones who would have to put up with them most often would be the staff."

Boston thought a moment. "You have a point, Laurel, you have a point."

"Just give it some thought." The screen went blank. His wallet buzzed. It was Jane Wayne. Squat, monocled and in her navy blue suit, she looked like a very dignified poison toad with all the reserve of two tectonic plates about to head butt. He had that effect on people.

"Why are you still alive?"

The screen went blank, his cue to turn up the heat. And he knew where to start.

Chapter 14

On the other hand, maybe it wasn't such a hot idea. James Cory's apartment was modest for a nano-chemist. It was sparsely furnished with mostly natural pine in livingroom, kitchenette and bedroom. There were a few interactive paintings on the walls. He said, "Winter" to one of them and it displayed a gentle snowfall on a quiet country road. The things they could do with nano-acrylics. Besides a workstation in one corner of the livingroom and a desk and bedside table in the bedroom, there wasn't much to search and what there was had turned up less. That had come from the bottom of the flip-top garbage can in the kitchen. It was a small glass case with glass seals, the kind of mini maximum containment container that might be used to carry nanobots. But then, James Cory had been a nano-chemist. On the other hand, the Lab Boys had found traces of nanobots-assembler bots-in Brandy's coffee, and Boston was certain that they would find the same in the others' coffee. If the Boys didn't come up with something, he'd have to make the coffee shop rounds again and get some more samples. But he was already a hundred percent certain that they would find the same thing.

And what was it with Dannyg breaking into Cory's computer? Cory had sensitive information that was no doubt given to him by Robert Gibson, information that Dannyg was likely using to develop "the good stuff." But how did he know to break into Cory's computer? There were over a thousand employees at Chaney. Breaking into all their accounts to find Cory's would surely have set of red flags all over the network. And how come Dannyg hadn't turned up as a statue in a coffee shop yet? Maybe he would soon. And what about Bob? How was Rob's argument buddy involved? Another piece of collateral damage like Brandy?

It was time. He took a deep breath, relaxed his shoulders, centered his awareness in his tan dien and his wallet buzzed. It was Laurel.

"Where are you, Boston?"

"Obviously not far away enough from everything keeping me from exploring the vibes."

"Give it up, Boston. You're just breaking your heart with that theory."

"What've you got for me?"

"James Cory's mysterious cell phone buddy."

She paused.

Boston waited.

She continued to pause.

It was too much for him. "Well?"

Laurel smiled a knowingly sardonic smile. "They were fake."

"Fake?"

"He was talking to dead air."

"All that up and down, loud and quiet, long streams of meaningless talk? He wasn't talking to anybody?"

"Looks like the cell phone was just a way of being an asshole."

"I think I heard that before."

"With the exception of three calls."

"And those?"

"Thelma Rice."

Boston let this piece of knowledge sink in for a moment. "So... it looks like Cory might have been in on whatever Thelma and Dannyg were cooking up. Or, they were in on whatever Cory and Gibson were cooking up. What we have here could be a meeting of chefs-four dead chefs and a snoopy librarian. I've got something for you." He scanned the inside of the glass container. "Found this in Cory's garbage. Looks like something that might be used to store nanobots."

"Think they might be the same as the ones in Brandy's coffee?"

"Hard to say. He was a nano-chemist. This might be the kind of thing they have lying all over the place." Glancing around the desolate room, though, he doubted that the container in his hand was something James Cory would have all over the place."

"Boston... "

"Do I sense a lecture?"

"No. I'm not going to berate you for breaking into James Cory's apartment without a warrant and going way too far with this referral that should have been made hours ago. I just want to inform you that Jane Wayne has stopped putting pressure on CI Central and whoever else she was hounding."

"I see-started doing things the Wayne Way. She called-asked why I was still alive. Is that some kind of probable cause?"

"It's cause for you to make your referral *toute suite*, before you're too dead to make it."

"The vibrations are with me. I'll be OK."

"You... "

He closed his wallet. *So, the four of them were in this together. And Brandy just stumbled in looking for a piece of whatever pie was being cooked up. And all five are dead.* But there were six of them in on it, and the sixth hadn't turned up dead yet. He knew it was time for a referral. He had enough to set one hell of a police investigation in motion. And that was about it. With Columbian coffee cartels, corrupt politicians, a legal industry based on addiction and Jane Wayne involved he knew that the investigation's wheels would be leaking air the moment they started spinning. They'd be flat in some desolate trash bin for punctured files before Earl had a chance to buy his coffee deco statues. He needed a referral with enough wind in it to keep the tires inflated.

He just had to stay alive long enough to deliver it.

Behind him, he heard the tiniest squeak as the door to James Cory's apartment opened. He had visitors.

Chapter 15

Two Columbians with perfect tans and almost blinding smiles strolled in, brimming with confidence, dressed in quietly flowered shirts and shorts. Not nearly enough splash for Boston's tastes. They took positions on either side of the door, standing there with gleaming machetes. Things were about to get interesting.

The one on the left introduced himself as Pedro. "And this is, Manuel. He's my associate, man." Manuel nodded. Everything about their demeanor exuded a thick layer of casually friendly icing over a cake full of razor blades.

"Manuel and I read about you all the time in the 'loids, man. It's a real pleasure to finally meet you. Least for us." The smile widened. "It makes us so sorry about this, man."

"And what would that be about?" asked Boston, just barely keeping his voice steady. Those machetes were about the most business-like instruments he'd seen since the one that had whizzed by his head earlier, and that had looked very business-like embedded in the wall at Lamb's.

In a movement so fast that Boston barely detected arm motion, Pedro threw his machete. But Boston was faster, twisting his head slightly with lightning speed. The machete flew by him in a blur and hit the wall behind him with a sickening thunk. "That?" he said, thumbing toward the machete.

"You one fast mother," said Pedro, not losing the smile for an instant. "But that's OK, man, we got more stuff." Manuel nodded and smiled wide. It was almost painful to look at those sparkling teeth. "By the way, what about them thirty naked pagan women in that Kilburn Blind Man case. You do them or somethin', man?"

"Just friends."

"Man, I'd do 'em. They lesbians or somethin'?"

"Or something." He breathed deeply, calming himself. "You know... killing a CI in the course of making a referral is punishable by up to five thousand hours of community work."

"That much, man? I didn't know that."

Boston looked at Manuel, giving him his most gravity-weighted CI stare. "And up to twenty-five hundred hours for an accomplice."

Manuel's smile widened.

Pedro reached his right arm around behind him. "Well, we got lots of stuff to do, man. Gotta get this over with." He brought his arm around, holding the biggest, shiniest gun that Boston had ever seen. With the silencer, it was almost big enough for Pedro to beat him to death with it, without having to step closer. It was a big gun.

Pedro lifted his arm and pointed the gun at Boston. "Man, I don't think you gonna duck this one."

Boston thought about the possibilities. They seemed suddenly limited. Should he dive to the left, the right, charge into the gun, do a backwards flip, jump straight up, beg for mercy and promise never to mess with Chaney Pharmaceuticals again? He watched Pedro's finger begin to pull on the trigger. *Better think of something soon.* And then, Pedro's finger seemed to loosen. He looked at the wrist phone on his left hand. "Gonna have to wait a minute to kill you, man. Gettin' a text." He read the message and looked up at Boston. "Must be your lucky day, man." He turned to Manuel and said something that Boston couldn't hear. Manuel slid his machete inside his shirt. Pedro put this gun back in his shorts.

Pedro turned back to Boston. "Hey man, since you ain't doin' them thirty pagan ladies, maybe you could pass me a number or two?"

"Sure, just leave me your contact info."

"Maybe I'll just be in touch." The two blinded Boston one more time with their smiles and left, closing the door quietly.

So, Jane Wayne wants me alive. Why?

And that's when it occurred to him.

They know about Dannyg and they don't know who he is.

Chapter 16

Boston liked park benches, especially the ones lining busy roadways with no parks around. Cars, buses and trucks streamed by honking horns, gearing up and down. But other than the horns, they were quiet, running on magnet lines buried under the streets. There were still the occasional fume spewers but they were getting less and less as the year-of-make moratorium took more of them off the roads each year. Pedestrians eyed him curiously, something in the back of their minds saying, "Is that really Boston Jonson from the webloids? Sitting there, right there, on a bench right in front me, right where I can go up and ask him about those thirty naked pagan women?" Another voice saying, "Naw, probably just a Boston Jonson wannabe dressed up like a webloid geek." That was OK with him. Busy streets with lots of activity relaxed him. The noise outside drowned out the noise in his head and allowed him to think more clearly, and he needed to think clearly.

Dannyg is the one who has whatever he needs to make the "good stuff." He's the only one not turned into stone. Or at least, as far as he knew. Maybe Dannyg's body just hadn't been discovered yet in one of the dozens of coffee shops in this part of town. Maybe Dannyg didn't drink coffee. Maybe he just made the "good stuff," and Boston was becoming increasingly certain that the good stuff was Columbian Red. Robert Gibson and James Cory were perfectly situated to tap into the dangerous brew's secrets, and Cory knew Thelma, who was working with Dannyg. It was all starting to fit together. And it looked like he had some breathing room, at least until he found Dannyg. Then it was anyone's guess.

His wallet buzzed. It was Jane Wayne.

"Haven't found him yet," he said and closed his wallet. The wallet buzzed immediately. It was Laurel.

"Boston. We know how they did it!"

"Did what?"

"Turn them into calcium."

She paused.

He hated it when she did that. But he waited. And waited. As usual, Laurel won. "How?"

She grinned. "Assembler bots... inside the assembler bots."

"Bots within bots?"

"You got it. The first layer of bots turn normal coffee into Columbian Red."

"Is that legal?"

"Highly illegal. But untraceable once their work is done."

"So how did we find them?"

"Under certain conditions the bots stray, like when they've been tampered with. And these ones were. They had a second bot inside. The Lab Boys managed to re-create the whole set. The one inside is a vicious little thing that just turned a cage full of rats into rodent statuettes. Cute little things, I'm told."

"How long did it take?"

"About five minutes for the bots to multiply and spread through their bodies, and then it was almost instantaneous. They didn't feel a thing."

"So it wouldn't have taken them much longer to spread through a human body?"

"Twenty minutes, tops."

"And the rats were on caffeine highs before they died?"

"A simulated caffeine high, Boston. The first layer of bots are programmed to go directly to the brain where they act similarly to caffeine as competitive inhibitors by binding themselves to adenosine receptors on the surface of cells without activating them... "

"Laurel?"

"I know... too much detail. You don't know what it's like to be interacting daily with these Lab Boys. I'll skip the pharmacology and get right to the nitty gritty. The caffeine high is a cover for the other things the bots do."

"Such as?"

"They make cocaine look like candy floss. And then they just disappear, turn themselves into water or something else that would normally appear in the brain."

"But there were some still in Brandy's coffee?"

"And that's where things get interesting. The container bots-the ones that give the coffee high-empty themselves from the cup into drinker's mouth as soon as the mouth touches the cup. They're attracted by saliva. Once inside the body, the assemblers break out and, as soon as they come into contact with calcium molecules, they absorb its chemical structure and multiply throughout the body until they reach a state of critical mass."

"And then they turn the entire body into calcium in a flash."

"Except nails and hair."

"And lipstick."

"Fast learner. Guess that's why you're in the webloids and I'm not."

"You know too much to be in the webloids."

"Last time I checked, Columbians weren't trying to slice and dice me with their machetes."

"Apparently, they don't want to slice me into stewing beef anymore. It seems that Jane Wayne's called them off."

"Why would she do that?"

"She wants me to stay alive."

"Again... why?"

"Dannyg."

"Dannyg?"

"They don't know where he is. They want me to find him."

"And then they slice and dice."

"That's my guess."

"And are you anywhere near to finding him?"

"Brick wall."

"Time for a referral?"

"Not yet."

"My advice?" She leaned in close to the cam. "Don't find him."

Boston laughed. "This is why you're not in the webloids. Talk to you later."

Dannyg. Where are you? And why are you the only one still alive?

A new thought began to curdle inside his head. *The only one still alive. Why is that?* And the curdling thought solidified. *Could you be the killer, Dannyg?* The solid shape of the thought began to turn in his head, showing its surfaces. Could he have gotten greedy? Maybe he didn't want to give "the good stuff" away to the hopped up caffeine masses. Maybe the dollar signs danced in front of his eyes and he decided to make himself a rich man. And maybe he wanted it all to himself. Maybe he didn't want any partners. But now he had even bigger problems than a few coffee addict partners. He had the Columbians after him.

Dannyg was going to be hard to find.

His wallet buzzed. It was Jane Wayne.

Chapter 17

The two men in light brown overcoats looked out of place sitting around the teak meeting table. They sat casually, quietly, their faces blank and unmemorable. About the only thing that might spark recognition five minutes after you passed either of them in the street would be their deep nasty eyes, and those eyes might drag you into dark places in your dreams. Even more disturbing, though, was Jane Wayne sitting behind her expansive desk like the Evil CEO of the Toads. She'd invited him in for a "reconciliation of diverse perspectives."

No one in the room had said anything yet. She'd gestured to the chair that Boston was to sit in. He was sitting in it. They were in a long ominous pause without the expectation of something revelatory and cool like the things Laurel tossed his way after her pauses. Jane Wayne sat with her hands clasped on her desk, staring into Boston's eyes. He breathed deeply, centering his chi, drawing calm from that vast storehouse of balanced energies in the air around him. It was almost working.

The corners of Wayne's wide amphibian mouth trembled and he wondered at what furnace of pure Boston Jonson-hating rage burned away behind that monocled eye. But she'd called the two Columbians off and there were better places to have him killed than her office. The two with the nasty eyes were likely there just for show. Or maybe they'd just kill him if this meeting didn't go right.

"As President of the Coffee Consultants and Coffee Shop Union... " She leaned forward about an inch, fixing her eyes somewhere inside Boston's eyes and right into the back of his head. She wasn't talking to him, she was talking through him. He wondered if it might be more comfortable to just have the two overcoats drop him out the window. "... I represent the local interests of those whose interests extend globally."

She let that sink in. Boston feared that this was going to be anything other than one of her short and terse conversations. He wanted her to just say, "You can go now."

No such luck.

"You're aware of Chaney Pharmaceuticals." Boston nodded yes. "I want you to tell me everything you know."

"About Chaney Pharmaceuticals? Well, they're a former legitimate drug company that... "

Her words flew at him like ice daggers. "About your referral."

"I'm sorry, but CI Central regards all information relating to a referral in progress as confidential... "

"No. It's not."

His wallet buzzed. It was Laurel. "Boston, orders from the top. Tell her everything." She signed off.

"Well?"

He shifted in his chair. What to tell her. What not to tell her. He sure as hell wasn't going to tell her everything. "Well, we have five dead people, all of them turned into calcium, apparently from assembler nanobots in their coffee."

Wayne glanced in the direction of the two men. They remained motionless, almost like the statues he'd been finding around the city, but they weren't calcium white.

Boston continued. "They were all Columbian Red addicts... "

"Consumers, Mr. Jonson. Not addicts. It's coffee."

He let it pass. "However, at the time of their deaths, they were drinking less... *consumer-oriented* coffees, which is strange given their overwhelming *consumer preference* for Columbian Red." Wayne glared into the back of his head. "From on-the-scene accounts, it appears that all of the victims were irritating people with a high probability of having many people who might want to see them dead."

Another glance at the men in overcoats.

"But I don't think it was like that."

The knuckles of Wayne's clasped hands were beginning to turn white. Terrible things brewed behind the monocle. "Two of the victims were former employees of Chaney Pharmaceuticals, James Cory and Robert Gibson. We have reason to believe they were collaborating in stealing confidential information, possibly concerning the manufacture of Columbian Red."

"Impossible," said Wayne. "It was developed in South America."

Lying evil toad. "It's likely they were stealing confidential information of some local nature.

Three other people were involved-Thelma Rice, a Free Coffee activist, Brandy Williams, a librarian who *consumed* Columbian Red and invited herself into whatever the others were doing, and Robert Howard. Haven't got a clue how he fits into it."

He paused to think about the information he'd given so far and considered how much more to give. Maybe just enough to singe a few feathers.

"I think they may have all been killed by a sixth person. Someone named Dannyg."

This brought a reaction. Boston was sure that the bones were going to split right through the skin on Wayne's knuckles. Judging from the movement under her navy blue jacket, her breathing was speeding up. The feathers were singeing.

"Apparently, Dannyg succeeded in replicating the process for... one of Chany's stronger blends of coffee. Something Thelma Rice referred to as 'the good stuff.'" Boston sank back into the chair. That was all the information he was going to give Jane Wayne.

"And?"

Or maybe just one more tidbit. "Apparently, every Magcab in the city is out to kill me."

Wayne didn't smile. He doubted that she ever smiled and, given the hideous smile that might curl around that wide frog-like mouth, this was probably a good thing.

"I have official information for you from Chaney Pharmaceuticals. Listen." Wayne lowered her clasped hands to her lap and leaned back in her chair, smug and self-assured. "James Cory was fired for having cybersex on the job with Thelma

Rice. Robert Gibson was fired for sexual harassment. Neither were stealing secrets from Chaney Pharmaceuticals. Whatever any of your victims were doing had nothing to do with Columbian Red. The person whose username is Dannyg was stealing low priority non-public information from James Cory's computer. Chaney Pharmaceuticals would like to employee a conflict resolution consultant for a non-antagonistic debriefing with him. You can go now."

***

Yep, they really want me to find Dannyg and they really want him dead. And me too probably.
At least now he knew what to look for.

Chapter 18

Yep, just as I suspected, he thought, looking at the two tiny glass containers in the palm of his hand. One had come from Rob's dirty jeans pocket. Getting it out had been less than the highlight of his day. Rob might be odorless calcium, but the stench of his live body still clung heavily to his clothing. Boston wondered if he smelled like this when he worked in security at Chaney. On the other hand, not a bad way to ward off anyone trying to steal deliveries from the runners. It had taken him a while to find Bob's container. He'd hidden it in one of his socks. Now he knew how the bots had gotten into their coffee. They'd put them in themselves. All five of them. Within hours of each other. They'd used themselves as lab rats, testing the "good stuff" without any thought of the possible side effects.

Addicts.

His wallet buzzed. It was Laurel.

"Got something about Robert Gibson. And Robert Howard."

Boston looked at the stone-frozen faces of Bob and Rob. Was he about to find out the connection between these two? Maybe even the reason they met here night after night to argue about everything under the sun-arguments so important to them that Bob would leave a date with the gorgeous Shelley to come here and fling words?

"They were brothers. Different fathers, same mother."

That would explain the arguments-sibling rivalry run amok.

"Thanks Laurel. As it happens, I'm with the two of them right now." He scanned the two glass containers with his wallet. "Got something coming in. Maybe get some nano trace from these."

"What are they?"

"I'm thinking they're the containers they used to carry the nanobots in."

Laurel thought about this for a moment, looking puzzled. Then she caught it. "You mean they did it to themselves?"

"Yep. All of them. Don't think they had a clue what was going to happen, but I'm sure they were their own guinea pigs. And Dannyg was the one who made the stuff. He would have to have known about the assembler bots. He put them in."

"He killed them deliberately? Why?"

"Sell the stuff and make a fortune."

"You believe that?"

"No."

"Then what?"

"There's a connection between James Cory and Dannyg that we're not seeing. James Cory was a nano-chemist. Dannyg has to be some kind of nano specialist to have made the assembler bots and put them inside the other bots."

"Are you thinking what I'm thinking, Boston?"

"Dannyg works for Chaney Pharmaceuticals."

"And they don't know who he is."

"They want me to figure that one out."

"But that would mean they might have been working on it together. Why would Dannyg be breaking into Cory's computer?"

"Haven't got that one figured out yet. Maybe to confuse anybody at Chaney who might be spying on employee mail. Maybe to stay one step ahead of Cory. Have we got Thelma Rice's address?"

"Forty-four Delaney Drive."

"That's only a couple of blocks away."

"Small world. You're not going to illegally break into her place, are you?"

"Can you get me a warrant?"

"How soon?"

"About ten minutes?"

"Don't get caught."

Chapter 19

No surprise. Thelma Rice's flat was dark, very dark. Black walls, with posters of CyberGoth musicians plastered everywhere at weird angles, some overlapping others. The furniture looked to be 20th Century Ghetto with black and gray throws. Metal and plastic gargoyles stared down snarling and grinning from shelves nailed to the walls and from the tops of tables and bookshelves. The bedroom was the same, black and infested with gargoyles. The floor was littered with clothing. One of two dressers - both painted black - spewed back bras, black underwear and black patterned hosiery from open drawers. One wall was completely covered with posters, plastered one over the other. The only white in the washroom was the toilet and the sink. The shower stall was black. The mirror over the sink was black, painted black, no reflection. He looked back in the bedroom. No mirrors attached to the dressers. Thelma Rice wasn't much for self-indulgence.

He made his way through the mess of clothing on the floor to the higher of the two dressers. The top was covered with small gargoyle statuettes. He opened the top drawer, the one most people filled with personal things. Thelma had lots of personal things: torn tickets for CyberGoth concerts, boxes brimming with metal rings and chains, interactive pictures of Thelma with friends dressed in black leather, form-fitting black outfits and tons of metal. Some of the men had collars around their necks with chains leading into the hands of women who looked like they'd just had cake and tea in Hell. One box contained about thirty keys. Boston had one of those boxes in his own top dresser drawer. Spread throughout the drawer were cosmetics cases and lipsticks... all of them black or zombie white.

The next drawer down was full of interactive pictures pretty much the same as in the top drawer. Going through them, he noticed that none of them were of Thelma in her earlier years, with family and childhood friends in times when she might have worn a flowered sundress. It looked like Thelma had said goodbye to all that. The next drawer down held old laptops and handheld devices, all made obsolete by her state-of-the-art crystal pendant holotop. The bottom drawer was empty. Or was it? He opened it a few inches more and discovered right at the back a small rubber duck. It was yellow. Something from Thelma's youth? A souvenir from a party? Something left there by the last owner of the dresser?

He liked to think that it came from her youth, one last vestige of her past that she couldn't bring herself to part with.

It occurred to Boston that he had no idea what he was looking for. One thing he was sure of-Thelma Rice was the link between Dannyg and James Cory. Cory had called her three times from his cell phone. Thelma knew that Dannyg had made the stuff and announced it on the Net. Was there something in her place that tied them all together, something that might be a clue to Dannyg's whereabouts, what his real name was?

He was sure the other dresser wasn't going to offer any clues. He waded through the clothing to the closet. The shelves were stacked with more clothing. No boxes full of clues, no telltale slips of paper, no diaries or journals-just stacks of dark clothing.

What am I looking for?

He looked around the bedroom. He knew there had to be something here. He could feel it. He made his way to the center of the room, almost stumbling on a tangle of chain laden clothing. He stood still, let his shoulders drop, let his awareness sink through his lungs and heart and into a quiet place just behind his belly button. He began to breathe deeply, right down to his toes, and exhale till there couldn't have been an iota of air left in his lungs and then breathed in deeply. Just as he was about to close his eyes, he saw it.

It was a pattern of linearity that didn't fit with the rampaging lines of the posters. There were three of them, straight lines, two parallel and one crossing the top of them. It was the outline of a door. He stepped carefully over to it. There was no visible knob or handle, but the crack in the wall was unmistakable. He reached out his hand and pushed lightly on it. It didn't budge. He tried digging his fingernails into one of the cracks. No luck. He tried the opposite crack. Same thing. He looked at the top crack and thought, no way. But he tried it anyway. The door moved very slightly away from the wall-enough for him to get a better grip and pull it right down. When it touched the floor, it became a ramp leading into what looked like a small room.

As he walked through the doorway, fluorescent lamps in the walls lit up.

In stark contrast to the rest of Thelma's flat, the walls in the secret room were spotless white. The room contained a single table and chair. Sitting on the table was a metal box about three feet high and three feet wide. Beside it, a remote holotop with two screens and a holoboard that appeared to have been left on. One of the screens displayed what looked like a ball of fiber. The other displayed what looked like the corner of a gray room. Boston touched one of the holokeys. Both screens went blank.

He took out his wallet and called Laurel.

"Boston, I hope you're somewhere legal."

"You don't want to know."

"Whatcha got?"

He pointed his wallet at the box and holotop and sent images to Laurel. "Haven't got a clue what this is, but maybe The Boys can come up with some ideas."

Laurel looked away from the screen for a moment as she said, "By the way, that glass container contained no nano... just some oozy stuff that the Lab Boys think was a coating for the nanobots. It would have dissolved in the coffee and... " She suddenly looked startled. She turned her head back to the screen. "Boston, this is a nano replicator."

"A what?"

"I authorized the purchase of one of these for The Lab Boys a few months ago. It's one of the pieces of equipment they've been using on your bot from Brandy's coffee. It's used to replicate nanobots. You put one in the box, run the program with the holotop and presto! You have as many bots as you want. You need special clearance to buy them."

"Like the kind of clearance a nano chemist might have?"

"He would need a spotless record, impeccable credit rating, untarnished background check and high level clearance from a reputable organization with its own high level clearance, and he still wouldn't be able to buy one. They're considered too dangerous for anyone to have their own personal nano replicator."

"But somebody who worked for Chaney Pharmaceuticals, that uses nano technology, might be able to get his hands on one?"

"You think it belonged to James Cory?"

"I think Cory and Gibson worked out a way to get it, and I think Cory wouldn't want it at his place. Too close to home."

"Boston, that *would* be home."

"I meant in the sense of too close to work, too close to scrutiny, too close to people with machetes, too close for comfort. Too close to home."

"Finished with your little tiff, Boston?"

"Yep. So, he used this to make the nanobots to recreate Columbian Red?"

"No."

"No?"

"That's just a nano replicator. It doesn't make things. It replicates them."

"So Cory would have needed some of the bots already made?"

"That's the way it works." Boston thought about this for a moment. "Thelma's posting said that Dannyg had *made* the good stuff. Maybe he passed that on to Cory for replication."

"They kept their operation in two places. All the better to foil the folks from Chaney."

"And Dannyg has the original bots. And the ability to make more of them."

"And he gave the deadly ones to Cory, knowing that he would pass them on to the others."

"And they couldn't wait to try them."

"So, where does that get us?"

"Right back to the question that keeps coming back-who is Dannyg? And where is he?"

"That's two questions."

"I have an idea."

"Going to break into somebody else's home?"

"Going to see somebody who might have some answers."

Chapter 20

After passing on another five books he'd never dream of reading, Boston climbed the stairs to the second floor of the library. The right side opened out to a high ceiling with stacks below on the main floor filled with CDs and DVDs. Ancient technology, but there were still those who used them. Hell, there were still people playing vinyl music. He wondered if there was still a company somewhere that made the equipment to play it- turntables, tone arms, needles and analog amplifiers. Was there a recording studio somewhere that sent tracks off to some secret operation deep in the recesses of Contemporary Nowhere that churned out limited edition vinyl records, those pre- digital things called albums?

The librarian he'd talked to earlier snapped her head in his direction as he stepped onto the shiny vinyl floor. The air smelled of flavored coffees. Young and old people milled about, seeming to not really be looking for anything in particular, going nowhere and emanating a disturbing quality of vacancy. He walked up to the librarian's desk. She looked strange in her rimless glasses. The top half of her head was a shiny glare, the bottom fitted with a tiny, puckered mouth that seemed out of place for the wide roundness of her head. Something in her eyes suggested impatience. He had that effect on people.

"Good crowd today," he said.

"It's good every day. Everything here is free." Her voice was flat, final, as though she'd said more than enough to make him go away.

"I was in earlier."

She sat and stared, her round eyes-made rounder and larger by the glasses-expressionless.

"I asked about Brandy Williamson."

Nothing. This was one tough nut.

He pulled out his wallet and opened it. "My name is Boston Jonson. I'm a CI assigned to a referral involving Ms Williamson." He pressed a few buttons in his wallet, brought up an image of Thelma and showed it to the librarian. "Have you seen this woman?"

Something registered in the librarian's eyes. What was it? Interest? Confusion? Excitement?

"I don't really approve of what that young woman has done to herself." Pontification. That's what was in her eyes. The passage of judgment. The leveling of others to her personal standards. "These CyberGoths are in for some serious wake up when they meet their maker."

"Then, you've seen her before?"

And now there was definitely excitement in her eyes. And then it hit him. Somebody was actually asking her questions. With everything automated through holotops and other forms of digital media, all of them easy to use even by young children (especially young children), the job of a librarian probably consisted almost exclusively of maintaining a database. These people who had once been among the most valuable sources of information in the world had been relegated to data

102

entry clerks. But now, this one had questions to answer-and she had the answers.

"Comes in here frequently. Usually stays an hour or so. Quiet and cooperative for her type. Why would a beautiful young woman like her shave her hair off? And now she's painted herself white!"

Boston closed his wallet. "Did you notice if she ever came in with someone? A man?"

She squinted her eyes and thought about this a moment.

"No. Always alone. She stays about an hour or so and then leaves. Alone."

She must have noticed the look of disappointment in his eyes. That was one thing she wouldn't want to see-disappointment in her inability to supply useful information.

"But," she said, "there is a particular young man who's always looking over at her. I don't think she even knows it. Never looks back at him. Too bad. He seems like a nice clean cut man who might be just the type to help her straighten herself out."

Something along the lines of elation must have been showing in his eyes because now her mouth curled into a moon-shaped smile. She had useful information.

"Can you describe him?"

She seemed almost excited now. "He only comes here in the evenings. He isn't at all like her. No piercings or metal hanging from his lips and eyebrows. He's sort of good looking, quiet, sandy brown hair. And he wears conservative colors, pressed slacks, checkered shirts, mostly short-sleeved... "

Short-sleeved? Checkered? Bells and buzzers sprang to life in Boston's head. He opened his wallet and pressed some buttons. He showed the image to the librarian. "Is this the young man?"

She looked and raised her eyes. "Oh my! He's painted himself white as well."

"This is the one who was staring at the young woman?"

"Yes, yes, that's him. But what's happened to him? He's always so... "

"Did you notice any other men eying her? Someone who might have come in only when she was here?"

Her round little mouth puckered, eyes squinting. She shrugged. "No. At least, not a lot. She's a beautiful young woman but she's bald and dripping with metal. She's the kind of person who's going to attract stares. But I can't think of anyone who might have given her more than passing stares, mostly out of curiosity."

Boston smiled, leaned over the desk, and patted her on the shoulder. "Thank you. You've been a tremendous help."

She beamed.

Boston hurried to the top of the stairs and called Laurel. "Keep this under the counter for now, but I think we've found him."

"Dannyg?"

"None other."

"Where?"

"Lamb's."

"But you've already been there. The only body you found was James Cory's... " Her jaw dropped. Her face froze. "You mean... ?"

"James Cory is Dannyg."

Chapter 21

"But that means that he was breaking into his own account."

"Or," Boston said, "using his computer at work as a conduit to the Chaney network."

"I'm not following."

"The workstations at Chaney are probably heavily monitored during working hours. Maybe not so much in the evenings, and that's when Cory was at the library. I don't think he was stealing information. I think he was disguising a personal order for the nano replicator."

"But when it was delivered... ?" Laurel eyes lit up. "Oh! Robert Gibson! He would have received it and channeled it... "

"Off site to some place where Cory could pick it up and move it to Thelma's place."

"But it's still just a replicator. He would still need the nanobots and, if the replicator is all the equipment he had, and if he didn't have access to any of the Columbian Red development at Chaney, then how did he get them?" A cloud of frustration drifted her face. "And why would he put the bots in his coffee, knowing that they would turn him into calcium?"

"Because he didn't know."

"There was someone else in their group?"

"No, not in the group. Someone outside. Someone who had access to the nanobots from Chaney."

"You mean someone who works for Chaney."

"Or somebody who represents Chaney's interests... locally."

His wallet buzzed. It was Jane Wayne.

Chapter 22

Sitting across the table from Jane Wayne, Boston wondered about this small but powerful woman. She seemed completely nonplussed, relaxed and in charge as she lifted the porcelain coffee cup to her wide red lips. She was one of those who sucked her coffee in, almost breathing it, to catch every bit of flavor. She left a lipstick mark on the cup that just seemed so Jane Wayne. She barely noticed the calcified body of Brandy Williams in the chair to her right.

They were at the Tenth Cup, the neutral ground that Boston had insisted where the meeting would take place. He was sure that he knew enough to have the Colombians kill him-ten times over, just to be sure.

"How did you know that I'd figured it out?" Boston lifted his own cup and sipped. They were both drinking normal coffee-he, the Belgium Chocolate; she, the regular blend.

"We've had the library monitored since we found learned about... " She glanced at Brandy. "... her. We overheard you telling your wallet that James Cory was Dannyg."

"I was talking to CI Central, not my wallet," he said, surprised that she was suddenly speaking normal English.

She stared across the table at him, expressionless.

"I've been instructed to tie up the loose ends with you so that you have nothing to be curious about. In turn, you'll be instructed by your superiors to bugger off."

"Sounds fair." The tables around them were packed. The quiet roar of conversations and people podcasting created a natural barrier of sound that ensured nothing that Jane Wayne or Boston said would be overheard. The two men in overcoats sat three tables away sipping cappuccinos from oversized mugs piled high with cinnamon topped froth. "How about if I tell it the way I see it and you just confirm it."

She almost cracked a smile. He was glad she didn't complete it. He wasn't ready for the image that would be etched into his memory from that frog-like mouth curling into a smile.

"James Cory, nano-chemist for Chaney Pharmaceuticals, was a *consumer* of Columbian Red. Robert Gibson, a security consultant for Chaney Pharmaceuticals, was also a *consumer* of Columbian Red. The two of them met at their mutual doctor's office and became friends, or maybe just cohorts. One or the other found out that Columbian Red was being developed mainly here. They hatched a plan to find out how it was made by breaking into the Chaney network and intercepting messages delivered through Gibson. One or the other-probably Cory, being a nano-chemist-found out about the nanobots in the coffee."

He waited for Jane Wayne to say something like, "Very observant of you, Mr Jonson." She didn't.

"Somewhere along the line, James Cory came into contact with Thelma Rice and fell in love with her. She became part of the plot."

He waited for Jane Wayne to raise an eyebrow. She didn't.

"Someone at Chaney Pharmaceuticals found out what Cory and Gibson were up to. Being addicts, they were probably sloppy."

He expected a smile of acknowledgement. Thank God it didn't come.

"They could have just killed the two, but they found out about Thelma and Dannyg. They didn't know for sure if Thelma was in on it and, because she was a very talented hacker, they didn't know how to find her because she hid her identity through layers of email accounts and usernames. Dannyg was a big mystery. They didn't know where he was hitting Cory's account from. That was likely with a lot of help from Thelma. They didn't know that both of them were operating just a couple of blocks away at the City Library."

He waited for a barely discernable look of disapproval. It didn't come.

"So, how to bring them all down? Even the ones they couldn't locate?"

He waited for a look of agreement. None came.

"Somebody came up with the bright idea of giving them a little present. Gibson was somehow tipped off that a shipment of the nanobots was coming in. Probably, he was told to watch for it. When it came, he helped himself to one or more of the nanobots. But these weren't just ordinary Columbian Red nanobots. These ones contained

110

assemblers that would turn the members of the gang into calcium statues-even the ones they couldn't track down. They even allowed Cory to obtain a personal nano replicator." He sat back in his chair. "That about sum it all up?"

Jane Wayne lifted the cup to her lips and aerosoled another shot of regular. Her mouth worked slowly as she savored the taste. "Does it to your satisfaction?"

"Just a couple of questions." Jane Wayne nodded the go-ahead with her eyes. "How does Chaney Pharmaceuticals plan to keep the nanobots a secret forever? Sooner or later, someone is going to stumble onto them."

She thought about this for a moment, sighed impatiently and said, "They don't have to. The use of nanobots in coffee will be legal in a few months. Chaney Pharmaceuticals has a powerful group of lobbyists working on it. It's practically a done deal."

"Unless there were a scandal... like the use of nanobots before they became legal. And having a group of people stealing the secret and giving it away free-I suppose that would make things problematic, stall the legalization for years, maybe forever."

She didn't comment.

"But one thing bugs me... "

She wasn't biting... just stared into the back of his head, the look magnified by that single round lens stuck to her eye.

"I don't think anybody at Chaney would murder anybody with nanobots. More likely they would torture them until they got the names of everybody in the group and then they'd just kill everybody."

Was that the minutest of twitches at the corner of that impossibly wide mouth?

"I think they allowed this one to be handled locally, by somebody representing their interests here."

Definitely a twitch.

"I guess my last question is... how did you know they would all use it at the same time. They could have tested it on one person first, maybe a cat or dog, a hamster."

Jane Wayne's eyes narrowed into angry little slits. "They were addicts."

That, thought Boston, was about the most he was going to get out of this referral.

***

"Yes, Laurel, I'm ready to make my referral."

The woman in the wallet radiated gladness. "Now we're in business! So, what's it gonna be? Police? Shaman? Addictive Substance Consequences Counselor? Art gallery? I kind of liked your idea about the National Geological Survey."

Boston laughed. "I was joking."

"I'm not. But that's me. Going to turn this one over to the police? Maybe a murder investigation?"

"No point. The whole thing would be covered up within hours. Like you said, they're powerful. They don't do community work for murder."

"So what then?"

"eBay. I know of one person already who's interested in buying two of the statues."

Laurel roared. And roared. He really liked her. When it passed, she breathed in deeply, exhaling in much the way Boston would when he was tuning himself in to the vibrations.

"So Boston, you risked your life on this one. What did you get out of it?"

He smiled. "An admission."

The words were barely out of his mouth before he jumped back just in time to miss being splattered by a Magcab.

THE END